Programming With C and Data Structure

Shivaprasad.KM

Invincible Publishers

First published in India in 2017 by Invincible Publishers

ISBN: 978-93-86148-31-5

Invincible Publishers
F-55, Sushant Lok II, Hong Kong Bazar Lane Sector 57, Guru- gram-122003

Opposite Kasturba Ashram, Radaur Distt Yamuna Nagar, Hary- ana- 135133

This book is dedicated to my family, friends and students

About the Author

Shivaprasad K M currently working as the Assistant Professor with the working experience of 6 years inDepartment of Computer Science and Engineering, Rao Bahadur Y Mahabaleshwarappa Engineering College, Ballari. He Holds M. Tech in Computer Cognition technology from Mysore university presently Pursuing his Ph.D. degree on the topic **Effective Pattern Discovery on Text Mining**in the Visvesvaraya Technological University Belagavi.He has attended several workshops and also published several research papers in the domain of Text mining and also other domains.Some among them are:

- K Means Clustering foce on Innovations in Information's,Embedded and Communication System- Nov 27 2015 ISBN No: 978-1-46738625-8.
- Text Mining: An Improvised Feature based Model Approach,IEEE Explore 2nd international Conference on Applied Theoretical Computing and Communication technology- 2016 21st to 23rd July 2016 978.
- Android based Moving Object Detection with Alert SMS with Image Streaming Institute for Exploring Advances in Technology International Journal of engineering Volume 1 Issue 1 July 2016,2016-17
- Google Glass Performance using Android and OHMD Technology IEAE Second International Conference on Advances in Engineering-2016 ISBN No:978-93-84698-23-2
- Cross Fertilization on Text Analytics, 104th Indian Science of Congress association January 3rd to 7th 2017.
- A Survey on Text Mining techniques and methods: A

Review Approach, Submitted the paper to SERSC: Science & Engineering Research Support Society Australia and its under review process

He his member of Indian science Congress association,Indian Science Technical education and IAEng. He also works for IEAE organisation as Reviewer and Member of international conference Papers.

Acknowledgement

Firstly, I would like to thank my Dad **Mr.Jagadesh Kalmutt** and Mom **Smt.Uma Devi Kalmutt** and all my **family members** for standing beside throughout the career by being my inspiration, motivation for continuing to improve my knowledge.

Speaking of encouragement, I would like to thank my beloved Professor **Dr. T Hanumantha Reddy**, Head of the Department, Department of Computer Science and Engineering, and our Principal **Dr.Hiregowdar Yerrannagoudaru** all the staff members of my department for their valuable support to my work.

I would like to thank our beloved chairman **Sri. Y Satish Reddy** Vice President and Chairman and **all Governing council Members** of Rao Bahadhur Y Mahabaleswarappa Engineering College Ballari and all **Management and Life time members** of VV Sangha Ballari for their valuable support.

I would like to extend my Thanks to **Dr.Gururaj Adoni** for his encouragement motivation and support with proper guidance to complete the book effectively with clear understandability for the students.

I would like to thank all my **relatives, friends, staff and students of Rao Bahadhur Y Mahabaleswarappa Engineering College** and many others whose names may not all enumerated. Their contributions mean a lot and acknowledge them whole heartedly.

Preface

This book has been written to make the students understand and enjoy learning C language. Book is useful to the one who is desirous in learning and developing C programs. It is especially designed for students studying under graduation for any engineering streams. Its aim is to replace the classroom learning.

Topics in this book are arranged module wise with examples for easy and effective learning. It includes module wise question bank for planned and smart learning for the examinations and to test the understanding of concepts discussed in each module. Wherever necessary, concepts are explained pictorially to facilitate easy grasping and better understanding. Along with the book, it includes lab manual also.

Hope you gain lot of knowledge from this book. Students with desire to improve their skills in programming find this book interesting and useful.

- Shivaprasad K M

Table of Contents

Module 1:

Introduction to C language

1.1 How to develop a program

A program can be developed using the two approaches, algorithm, pseudocode, and flow chart. An algorithm is the systematic approach to develop the program for getting the desired output. This developed algorithm can be represented using the pseudocode and flowchart.

1.1.1 Algorithm:

An Algorithm is a finite sequence of unambiguous steps to describe the programming logic, where each step is numbered hierarchically. Steps must be complete and error-free. The steps must specify the input and output as per the requirement of the user. Steps in the algorithm should terminate, it cannot be open ended.

Example: Algorithm to calculate the addition of two numbers.

Step 1: Start

Step 2: Read two numbers A and B.

Step 3: Add the numbers A and B and store in C.

Step 4: Display C.

Step 5: Stop.

1.1.2 Pseudocode:

Pseudocode is the informal method of describing and representing the program. Pseudo means imitation and code means instructions which is written in the programming languages. Pseudocode does not obey any syntax rules, it just represents the basic structure of the actual program.

- ✓ Pseudocode allows the programmer to focus on the logic of algorithm without being distracted to the language syntax.
- ✓ The Pseudocode can be easily translated to any computer code. Even the less experienced can also easily do the translation.
- ✓ Pseudocodes are more concise, readable, easy to modify. Hence, allow programmers to easily design and develop the program the pseudocode.

Example:

begin

input: two numbers A and B

process: Perform addition of two numbers A and B, store result in C.

output: Result of addition C.

end

1.1.3 Basic Structure of C program:

Every programming languages have their own different format of coding. For C, the basic components required are:

- Preprocessor directives.
- global declaration of variables or functions.
- main( ) function section.
- pair of curly braces { }.

- declaration and statements.
- user defined functions.

i. **Preprocessor directives**: Precprocessor directives which are also called as precompiler directives are the special instructions used to tell how the complile the program. These statements begin with #symbol. Most important pre-processor directive is **include,** direct the pre-processor to include the header files. The **define** is also used to assign any constant values to symbolic constants in the program.

eg.,

#include<stdio.h>

#include<math.h>

#define MAX 100

ii. **Global declaration of variables or functions**: Declaring the variables or functions outside of all the functions including main( ) function is called global variables and their declaration is called global declaration. They are accessible from all the functions and decalred before the main( ) function.

iii. **main( ) function section:** As the name implies, it is the main function of the C program.Program may contain any number of functions with one and only main function. The exection of the program starts from this main( ) function.The function name is wriiten in lowercase 'main( ) and not terminated by any semicolon.

iv. **Pair of curly braces { }:** Program execution begins from the opening curly braces. The left curly brace indicate beginning of main function and right brace, indicates the end of main function. The braces are also used to indicate beginning and end of other user defined functions.

v. **Declaration and statements:** All the variables, arrays, functions are declared and they can also be initialized using the data types. Statements are the instructions to perform the specific operations. The statements can be I/O statements, arithimetic statements, control statements etc.,

vi. **Comment lines**: Comments are the explanatory notes, enclosed within /* . . . . */. These comment lines are not compiled and executed.

vii. **user defined functions:** User defined functions are written to perform specific task. These functions are written by user, hence the name user-defined. They can be written before or after the main function.

eg.,

```
#include<stdio.h> /*Preprocessor directives*/

void main() /*main function*/

{               /*curly braces*/

int a=1, b=2,c; /*declaration and intialization*/

c=a+b;

printf("result=%d",c);

}
```

1.2 Basic Concepts of C

1.2.1 Character Set:

In C programming, characters play the crucial role. They act as building blocks to form a basic lexical C program element such as constants, variables, operators, expressions etc., Character set uses alphabets, digits, certain special characters and whitespaces.

Following table shows the entire character set:

Uppercase Letters	A B C D E F G H I J K L M N O P Q R S T U V W X Y Z
Lowercase Letters	a b c d e f g h i j k l m n o p q r s t u v w x y z
Digits	0 1 2 3 4 5 6 7 8 9
Special Characters	
Comma	,
Period	.
Semicolon	;
Colon	:
Question mark	?
Apostrophe	‘
Quotation mark	“
Underscore	_
Hash/Number sign	#
Dollar sign	$
Percentage sign	%
Pipeline character	|

Slash	**/**
Backslash	****
Ampersand	**&**
Tilde	**~**
Caret	**^**
Asterisk	*****
Plus sign	**+**
Minus sign	**-**
Less than	**<**
Greater than	**>**
Left parenthesis	**(**
Right Parenthesis	**)**
Left Bracket	**[**
Right Bracket	**]**
Left Brace	**{**
Right brace	**}**

1.2.2. Tokens

Tokens refer to the smallest unit of C program. C program is composed of lexical elements, these elements are characters and white spaces that are grouped together into tokens. Tokens in C are :

- Identifiers.
- Keywords.
- Constants.
- Operators.

1.2.2.1 Identifiers

Identifiers are the names provided to the elements of C program such as, variables, functions, and arrays.

eg., n, _id, abc1, a_b_1.

Rules for defining identifiers:

- An identifier may consist of letters, digits, and special character underscore (_).
- An identifier must not have any special character except underscore.
- An identifier should start with letter or underscore only.
- An identifiers are case sensitive.
- An identifier cannot have reserved keywords.
- An identifier must not have two consecutive underscores.

1.2.2.2 Keywords

Keywords are the reserved words that cannot be used while naming a variable or function. They have predefined special meaning which are used for particular intended purpose. Keywords cannot be used as identifiers.

Following table shows standard keywords with their description:

Keywords	Description
auto	Defines a local variable having local lifetime
Break	Allows to pass the control out of block
Case	Used in switch statements to mark blocks of text.
char	refers to data type that holds character

const	used to define constants
continue	sends control back to top of a loop
default	specifies the default block of code in a switch statement.
Do	starts a do-while loop.
double	refers to a data type that holds 64 bit floating point numbers
else	indicates an alternative branch in the if statement
enum	refers to class of constants that represents fixed choices
extern	indicates that an identifier is defined elsewhere.
float	represents single precision floating point data type.
For	provides iteration facility repeatedly
goto	used to jump the control from one part of program to another
If	used to execute specified statements if the specified condition is true.
Int	refers to data type that holds integer type values.
long	refer to data type that holds the long type values.
register	informs the compiler to store the variable that is declared in a CPU register.
return	returns the value to calling function
short	refers to type modifier.
signed	refers to type modifier that holds the signed type values of a data type.
sizeof	returns the size in bytes of a specified parameter.

static	preserves the value of a variable even after its scope ends.
struct	Groups variables in a single record.
switch	represents multiple branching statement
typedef	assigns symbol name to data type definition
union	groups the variables sharing the same storage space.
unsigned	refers to the type modifier that holds the unsigned type values of a data type
void	represents the empty data type
volatile	indicates that variable can be changed by background routine.
while	represents the execution of a block, if the condition remains true.

1.2.2.3 Constants

Constants are the values assigned to variables which cannot be modified during execution of a program. They can be number, character, or a character string. Constants are also known as constant literals. Constants are defined by using the keyword **const.**

There are four basic types of constants in C:

i. Integer constants.

ii. Floating point constants.

iii. Character constants

iv. String Constants

i. **Integer constants:** It represents the whole number. It can be decimal, octal, or hexadecimal numbers. It displays the sequence of digits without any decimal point. It can be prefixed by plus or minus. eg., 2100, +15, -96.

ii. **Floating point constants:** It represents the numbers with decimal part. It consists of integral part, decimal point, fractional part, exponent part and optional suffix. Both the integral and decimal part contains decimal digits eg., 2100.6, +15.2, -96.6, 0.45, 1E+5, 7.32-5.

iii. **Character constants:** A character constant represents the single character enclosed within the apostrophe ' '. eg., 'n', ';', '6'.

iv. **String constants:** A string constant or literal represents zero or more charcaters enclosed in double quotation marks. eg., "Hello".

1.2.2.4 Operators

Operator is used to perform some operation. Any expression consists of an operator and operand. An operator acts upon the operand. There are three types of operators:

- Unary operators
- Binary Operators
- Ternary Operators

1.3 Data Types

A data type is type of data which is specified at the time of declaration of variable. It is used to define the type of data that is stored in the variable. The value of variable can be of data type. Data type determines the amount of storage required and that must be allocated to a variable. In C, there are many built-in data types.Following table shows the different built-in data types.

Types	Keyword	Description	Size in bytes	Range
integer	int	Stores the whole numbers	2	Signed -32768 to +32767 Unsigned 0 to 65535
floating point or real	float	Stores real numbers that has single prescision floating point.	4	3.4 e-38 to3.4 e+38
Character	char	Stores the single character.	1	Signed -128 to +127 Unsigned 0 to 255
Double precision floating point	double	Stores real numbers that has double prescision floating point.	8	1.7e-308 to 1.7e+308
Non-specific	void	stores no value	-	

a) **The int data type:**

This data type is used to store the integer value or whole numbers in a variable. Range of an int data type depends on the word length defined for the computer. In 8–bit computer, range of int data type is -2^{8-1} to $+2^{8-1}-1$ ie., -128 to +127. Similarly 16-bit computer has range from -32768 to +32767.

eg., int a;

Here, a is the variable name which can store integer value.

The following table shows some of the valid and invalid integers:

Valid Integer	Invalid Integer
-228	-34.0 (decimal point not allowed)
1780	1,533 (comma not allowed)
+180	999999999 (Out of range)
0	12,52.93 (comma and decimal point not allowed)

b) **Float data type:** This data type is used to store the real values in a variable. It stores the single precision floating point numbers. The numbers can be expressed either in the decimal notation or scientific notation. The numbers contain the decimal point wither to left or right of an integer. The scientific notation, mantissa-exponent notation.

eg., float a;

Here, a is the variable name which can store real value.

Valid	Invalid
-228.58	-3.4.2 (two decimal points not allowed)
1780.54E+3	1,533 (comma not allowed)
0.180E+2	-999999999.99 (Out of range)
2365.46E-2	-+23.43 (two successive operators not allowed)

c) **Character data type:** This data type is used to store some text or alphabetical information in a variable. The keyword used to define this data type is **char**.It stores either character or string constant and takes 1 byte for storage. A character constant is a single character enclosed between pair of single quotes. A string constant is a sequence of characters enclosed within a pair of double quotes. String constant should always be terminated by null character (\0).

eg., char ch, alpha;

ch='A' // character constant

alpha="String"; // string constant

d) **Double data type:** This data type is used to store numerical information in a variable. The keyword used to define this data type is **double**. Double data type is mainly meant for real values. It is same as float data type, but capacity is larger than float data type. It is used when the more accuracy is required in representing the floating point numbers. Float data type stores 6-digits after decimal point whereas, the double stores 16 digits after decimal point.

eg., double val;

e) **void data type:** The void data type does not store any values, therefore we cannot perform operations on the variables declared as void. The void data type does not have neither size nor any permissible range. This data type is typically used to return in a function that contains no return value. When the function does not return any value, you can declare the return type as void.

1.4 Variables

A variable is an identifier used to represent the specified type of information. The value of a variable may change during execution, but, the data type associated with that is not changed. These are the names provided to values to identify the programming elements. They refer to a specific location in the memory where data can be stored easily. The name is associated with the memory location of type integer, or float, or character etc.,

Each variable has a name and data-type. All the variables must have their type indicated so that compiler can record all necessary information, generate appropriate code during translation and allocate the required space in the memory.

Naming conventions for variables:

- Avoid the usage of capital letters in variable names.
- Use an alphabet or an underscore as a first character of a variable name and all the succeeding characters as letters and digits.
- Do not use commas, blank spaces, keywords and special characters to name variables.

1.4.1 Declaring Variables

Variable must be declared before it can be used. They are declared so that amount of memory is already reserved for the variable. Variables can be declared at start of any block of code, usually declared at start of function. Local variables are created when function is called and destroyed on return from that function.

Syntax: data_type variable_list;

where,

data_type refers to any built-in data type.

variable_list refers to list of one or more variables of data_type.

example:

```
#include<stdio.h>

void main()

{

int a, b,c; /*declaration */

printf("enter the value of a and b");
```

```
scanf("%d%d", &a,&b);

c=a+b;

printf("result=%d",c);

}
```

1.4.2 Intializing Variables

Once the variable has been declared, next value is assigned to the variable. This process of assigning the value to variable is called as initialization of a variable. The variables hold some memory location where the data can be stored. Value is stored in the variable using the assignment operator.

Syntax of initializing the variable is

variable_name=value;

where,

variable_name refers to name of variable where the value is stored actually.

value refers to the value that is used to initialize the variable.

example:

```
#include<stdio.h>

void main()

{

int a=5, b=10,c; /*Intialization */

c=a+b;

printf("result=%d",c);
```

```
}
```

1.4.3 The Printf( ) Function

Printf( ) function is used to display the information on the screen. It returns number of charcaters printed by printf( ) function or a negative value if an output error occurs.

Syntax: printf("control character", variable_list);

where,

control character determines the type and format values to be displayed.

variable_list is the list of variables that you want to display.

Printf( ) place holders

Place holders are used to print the values of arguments specified in printf( ) function. The general form is :

% flag field-width precision prefix type-identifier

Type identifier specifies the type of value to be displayed. **Following table shows the different type identifiers with their description:**

Type-identifiers	Description
d,i	Represents Signed integers.
o	Represents unsigned integers displayed in octal form.
u	Represents unsigned integers displayed in decimal form.
x	Represents unsigned integers displayed in hexadecimal form and hexadecimal characters such as a,b,c,d are printed in lowercase.

X	Represents unsigned integers displayed in hexadecimal form and hexadecimal characters such as A,B,C,D are printed in uppercase.
c	Converts any value to an unsigned char and displays it. It is used for rinting characters.
s	Converts the argument into character array and prints it, last null in string is not printed.
f	Prints floating point.
e,E	Represents the floating point in exponential form. It has one digit to the left of decimal point, the number of digits n right side of decimal point depends on the required precision.
g,G	Prints the floating point in exponential form. The exponential form is used if the exponent is less than -1. However both are slightly different in functionality.
n	Prints the number of characters, which are printed soo far by printf function
p	Specifies the value of a pointer.

1.4.5 The scanf( ) Function

The scanf( ) function is the formatted function used to read the input from the standard input device such as keyboard. The scanf( ) function is used to enter numeric that contains first string argument and it may have additional arguments. The syntax of scanf( ) function is scanf("control character", address_list);

where

control character is sequence of one or more control characters, it decides the type of values that are to be provided to variables. Control characters are preceded by % sign.

address_list represents the address of memory location where the memory values of input variables are to be stored.

scanf( ) place holders

The scanf( ) place holders contains % at beginning and type indicator at end. The general

Type indicator is a character specifying the type of data to be read. **Following table shows the different type indicators with their description:**

Type Indicator	Description
d,i	Reads the signed integers the expected argument should be pointer to int
O	Reads the unsigned integer in octal form
U	Reads the unsigned integer in decimal form
x,X	Reads the unsigned integer in hexadecimal form
E,e,f,g,G	Reads the floating point values.
S	Reads character string. It matches the sequence of non-white space characters terminated by end of line or end of file character.

C	Matches the number of characters according to a specified width. If no width is specified, single character is assumed as field width.
N	Writes the number of characters so far in the target variable but it does not read any input

1.5 Operators

An Operator is used to perform some operation. Any expression consists of an operator and operand. An operator acts upon the operand. The operators are used to operate not only on numbers but also on data variables. There are three types of operators:

i. Unary operators

ii. Binary Operators

iii. Tertiary Operators

i. **Unary Operators:** The operators that act upon the single operand to produce the new value are known as unary operators. The most commonly used unary operators are,

a) minus operator –

b) increment operator + +

c) decrement operator - -

d) sizeof( ) operator

e) (type) operator.

 Minus operator –

The common unary operator is unary minus, where the

numerical constant, variable or expression is preceded by a minus sign. It is distinctly different from the arithmetic operator which denotes subtraction.

eg., -12, -x, -(a+b).

- **The Increment and Decrement operators**

  The increment operator adds 1 to operand, whereas decrement operator subtracts 1 from operand. The increment and decrement operators can be used in two different ways, depending on whether the operator is written before or after operand.

- If the operator precedes the operand, then it is called a **pre-increment operator.** Value of operand is changed before it is used for its intended purpose within the program. eg., ++a;

- If the operator follows the operand, then it is called a **post-increment operator.** Value of operand is changed after it is used. eg., a++;

example: Program to demonstrate pre-increment and post-increment.

```
#include<stdio.h>
void main( )
{
int a, b;
a=5;
b=10;
/* Preincrement*/
printf(" Value of a: %d", a);
printf(" Value of a++: %d", a++);
printf(" New value of a: %d", a);
/* Post-increment*/
printf(" Value of b: %d", b);
printf(" Value of ++b: %d", ++b);
```

```
printf(" New value of b: %d", b);
```

Output:

Value of a : 5
Value of a++: 5
New value of a: 6
Value of b : 10
Value of ++b: 11
New value of b: 11

Size of Operator

An operator sizeof is used to calculate size of various datatypes. These datatypes can be basic or primitive data types. sizeof operator looks like function, but it is actually an operator that returns length, in bytes. If the type name is used, it should be always enclosed in parenthesis, whereas name can be specified with or without parenthesis.

example: Program to demonstrate sizeof operator.

```
#include<stdio.h>
void main( )
{
int i;
char c;
printf(" Integer %d", sizeof i);
printf(" Character %d",sizeof c);
printf("Integer %d", sizeof(int));
printf("Float : %d", sizeof(float));
printf("double: %d", sizeof(double));
```

Output:

Integer 2

Character 1

Integer 2

Float 4

Double 8

ii. **Binary Operators:** The operators that act upon the two operand to produce the new value are known as binary operators. The most commonly used binary operators are,

a) Arithmetic Operators.

b) Assignment Operators

c) Relational Operators.

d) Logical Operators.

e) Bitwise Operators

f) **Arithmetic Operators**

In most of programs, for solving the problems we need to perform arithmetic operations by writing arithmetic expressions. The different arithmetic operators in C are +, -, *, \, and %. Each operator manipulates the two operands, which can be constants, variables or other arithmetic expression. The remainder or modulus % operator is used to return the remainder value after dividing two integers. The % can be used for float or double data type.

Precedence Rules:

- Unary operators -, + are evaluated.
- Multiplication and division operators are evaluated.
- The addition and subtraction operators are evaluated.
- The assignment operator is evaluated.
- The expression is evaluated from left to right.

example: Program to demonstrate arithmetic operators

```
#include<stdio.h>
main()
{
int a,b,c,d;
int sum, sub,mul,rem;
float div;
printf("enter the values of a and b\n");
scanf("%d%d",&a,&b);
sum=a+b;
sub=a-b;
mul=a*b;
div=a/b;
rem=a%b;
printf("sum=%d, Sub=%d, mul=%d, div=%f, rem=%d, sum,
sub, mul, div, rem);
}
```

g) **Assignment Operator**

Assignement operator assigns the value of expression on the right side to the variable on left side of it. The equal sign (=) is the assignment operator.

The general form of assignment operator is ,

var=expression

where,

var is variable for which the new value is assigned.

expression represents the constant

eg., a=10; a=b+c;

- **Note:** When the two operands in an assignment operator are of different data types, the value of the expression on the right side of operator will be automatically converted.

- **example:**

```
#include<stdio.h>
main()
{
int a,b,c,d;
printf("enter the values of b,c, and d\n");
scanf("%d%d%d",&b,&c,&d);
a=b+c*d;
printf("a=%d",a);
}
```

h) Relational Operators

In C, the relational operators are used to compare or test the relation between two entities. The relational operators return true or falsed depending upon the condition the two entities hold. The Zero indicates false and non-zero is taken as true. Thefour relational operators are, <, <=, >, =. And there are two quality operators == and !=.

Relational Operators	Meaning
<	less than
<=	less than or equal to
>	greater than
>=	greater than or equal
==	equal to
!=	not equal to

example : Program to demonstrate relational operators

```
#include<stdio.h>
main()
{
int a=5, b=10;
```

```
if(a==b)
printf("a and b are equal");
if(a!=b)
printf("a and b are not equal");
if(a<=b)
printf("a is less than or equal to b");
if(a>=b)
printf("a is greater than or equal to b");
}
```

i) Relational Operators

In addition to the arithmetic and relational operators there are logical operators, they combine the logical values and create the new logical value. There are three logical operators :

Logical Operator	Meaning
!	NOT
&&	Logical AND
||	Logical OR

NOT: NOT operator is unary operator, it changes the true value to false and false value to true.

AND: The AND && operator is the binary operator, its result is true only when both the operands are true; Otherwise it is false.

OR: The OR|| operator is the binary operator, its result is false only when both the operands are false; Otherwise it is true.

j) Bitwise Operators

The bitwise operators are bit manipulation operators. It assumes operands as string of bits and bit operation is done on these operands. There are 6 bitwise operators: AND(&), OR(|), XOR(^), complement (~), left shift (<<), right shift (>>).

Operator	Explanation
&	Compares each bit of first operand to corresponding bit of second operand. If both bits are 1, then corresponding result is set to 1, otherwise set to 0.
|	Compares each bit of first operand to corresponding bit of second operand. If either of bit is 1, then corresponding result is set to 1, otherwise set to 0.
^	Compares each bit of first operand to corresponding bit of second operand. If one bit is 0 and the other is 1, then corresponding result is set to 1, otherwise set to 0.
~	Complements every bit of the operand
<<	shift their first operator to its left
>>	shift their first operator to its left

example: Program to demonstrate bitwise operators

```
#include<stdio.h>
main()
{
int a=5, b=10;
a=a>>3
printf("The value of a is =%d", a");
b=b<<3
printf("The value of b is =%d", b");
}
```

iii. **Ternary Operators:** The operators that act upon the three operands to produce the new value are known as ternary operators. The ternary operator used is conitional operator (? :). The syntax: **e1? e2: e3;**

First, the e1 is evaluated which if true, and then e2 is executed. If e1 is false, then e3 is executed.

example: Program to demonstrate conditional operator

```
#include<stdio.h>
main()
{
int a=5, b=10;
int result1, result2;
result1=a>b?a:b;
printf("The value of result1 is =%d", result1");
result2=a<b?a:b;
printf("The value of result2 is =%d", result2");
}
```

Output:

The value of result1 is 0
The value of result2 is 1

Questions:

1. Briefly explain the history of C.
2. Explain the basic structure of C program.
3. What are identifiers. List the rules to define the valid identifiers.
4. What are keywords?
5. What are constants? List various types of constants with example.
6. Explain the various data types supported by C.
7. What are operators. How to classify C operators?
8. Explain different types of operators with example.
9. Write a C program to calculate area and perimeter of the circle.
10. Write a program that takes 4 numbers and output the average.
11. Write a C program to find the simple interest.
12. Write a C program to check whether given number is odd or even.

Module 2:

Branching and Looping

Any expression can become a **statement** if it is followed or terminated by the semicolon (;). The Semicolon is called the statement terminator.
eg., a=1;

x=a+b+c;

2.1 Different Types of Statements:

C language provides three different types of statements, simple statement, compound statement, and control statement. A **Simple statement** is a simple single instruction ending by semicolon. A **Compound Statement** is group of multiple statements within the { and }.

Control Statement is the statement which controls the flow of execution of the statements generally called as control structures. These statements can be either conditional statements or iterative statements.

- **Conditional Statements:** These statements are also called **decision making or branching** statements. This statement involves one or more conditions to be evaluated to evaluate the following group of statements. Control statements can be if, if-else, nested-if, switch statement.

- **Iterative Statements:** These statements are also called **looping statements.** We may have the number of situations where it may be required to execute the certain statements repeated for known number of times or until the specified condition is met. Iterative statements can be while, do-while, for.

2.1.1 Conditional Statement:

In the control statements first the specified conditional expression is evaluated. Once the evaluated expression comes out as true, the following statements are executed. If the conditional expression comes out to be false the following statements are skipped. This is called as conditional execution. Conditional execution involves both decision making and branching.

The Typical control structure model is as below:

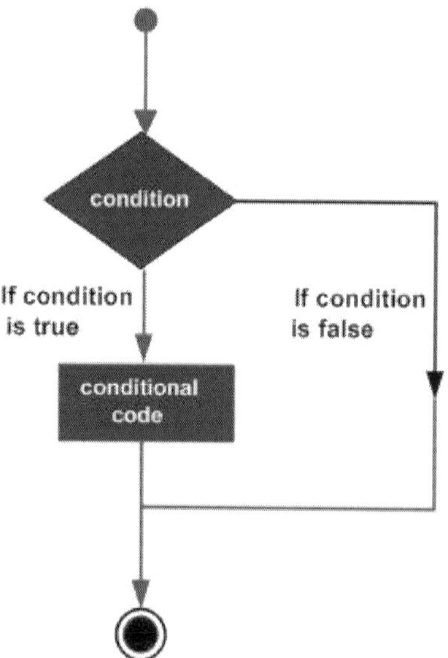

Note : C language assumes any non-zero or non-null value as **true** and zero or null is assumed as **false**.

Conditional statements involve different types of selections:

- **One-way selection**: In this if the condition is evaluated to be true, then the statements in the true block are executed else they are ignored and control is transferred to next statements in the sequence. An Example of one way selection is **if statement** without any else statement.

- **Two way selection**: In this if condition is evaluated to be true, then the statements in true block are executed else the statements in the false block are executed. An example of two-way selection is **if-else statement**.
- **N way or Multiway Selection**: In this conditional expression has the multiple values to be tested. An example of this **switch statement**.

Hence let us discuss different types of conditional statements:

- if statement
- if-else statement
- nested if-else statement.
- Cascaded if-else statement.
- switch statement.
- Nested switch statement.

1.1.1.1 If Statement:

- This is simple decision making statement.
- It is also called as one way branching.
- Here, the conditional expression is evaluated.
- Simple or compound statements within the block of ' **if** ' are executed if the conditional expression turn to be true. Otherwise, control is next executable statements.
- The Conditional expression is enclosed between the parenthesis. It can be constant, variables, logical comparisons.

Syntax:

```
if(condition)

Statement;

or

if(condition)

{

Statement 1;

Statement 2;

Statement 3;

.

.

.

Statement n;

}
```

Flow chart:

Example programs:

1. Write a C program to accept a number and print if it is even number.

```
#include<stdio.h>

void main()

{

int num;
```

```
printf("enter the number \n");
scanf("%d",&num);
if((num%2)==0)
printf("%d is a even number",num);
}
```

Output:

```
enter the number
10
10 is a even number
```

2. Write a C program to accept floating point numbers and compute their ratio. If ratio is greater than zero then it should exchange the contents of input numbers.

```
#include<stdio.h>
void main()
{
    float x,y,ratio,temp;
    printf("enter x and y\n");
    scanf("%f%f",&x,&y);
    ratio=x/y;
    printf("ratio=%f",ratio);
    if(ratio>0)
    {
```

```
        temp=x;
        x=y;
        y=temp;
    }
    printf("x=%f,y=%f",x,y);
}
```

Output:

enter the value of x and y

16

4

ratio= 4.0

x=4,y=16

1.1.1.2 **if-else statement:**

- In the case of if statement, it executes only one action.
- Here, the conditional expression is evaluated.
- If the condition evaluated is true then true block statements (simple or compound) immediately following the if statement are executed. Otherwise, the false block statements in the else part are executed.
- In either case only one block of statements are executed but not both.
- After the executing the if-else, subsequently control is

transferred to next following statements of if-else structure in the program.

Syntax:

```
if(condition)
Statement;
else
statement;
or
if(condition)
{
Statement 1;
Statement 2;
Statement 3;
.
.
Statement n;
}
else
{
Statement 1;
Statement 2;
```

```
Statement 3;
.
.
Statement n;
}
Statement;
```

Flow chart:

Example programs:

1. Write a C program to accept a number and print if it is even number or odd number.

```
#include<stdio.h>
void main()
{
int num;
printf("enter the number \n");
scanf("%d",&num);
if((num%2)==0)
    {
    printf("%d is a even number",num);
    }
    else
    {
```

```
        printf("%d is a odd number",num);
        }
    }
```

Output:

enter the number

10

10 is a even number

enter the number

9

9 is a odd number

2.1.1.3 Nested if-else statement

- If it is required to select more than two alternatives then nested if-else can be used.
- This is also called as multi-way selection.
- if-else statement enclosed between another if statement is called as nested if-else statement.
- Control is transferred to inner if-else statements only when outer if statements is evaluated to be true.

Syntax:

```
if(condition1)
{
    If(condition2)
    {
    Statement 1;
    }
```

```
        else
        {
        Statement 2;
        }
    }
    else
    {
    Statement 3;
    }
    Statement;
```

Flow chart:

Example programs:

1. Write a C program to accept a three numbers and print the largest number.

```
#include<stdio.h>
void main()
{
int a,b,c;
printf("enter the three numbers");
scanf("%d%d%d",&a,&b,&c);
if(a>b)
{
        if(a>c)
        printf("a is largest number=%d",a);
        else
        printf("c is largest number=%d",c);
}
else if(b>c)
        printf("b is largest number=%d",b);
else
        printf("c is largest number=%d",c);
}
```

Output:

enter the three numbers
10
5
6
a is largest number=10

1.1.1.3 Cascaded if-else statement

- Putting together multiple if-else statements in sequence for involving multiple decisions is called cascaded if-else statement.
- It is chain of multiple if's asscociated with each else.
- This is also called as else-if ladder.
- Condtional expression is evaluated from the top in sequence. As soon as condition expression evaluates to be true it executes its corresponding statements and skips the remaining else-if statements.

Syntax:

```
if(condition1)
Statement 1;
clsc if(condition2)
statement 2;

else if(condition n)
statement n;
else
default statement;
```

Flowchart:

Example Programs:

```
#include<stdio.h>
#include<conio.h>
```

```
int main()
{
char alpha;
clrscr();
printf("enter an alphabet\n");
scanf("%c",&alpha);
if(alpha='a')
printf("It is vowel");
else if(alpha=='e')
printf("It is vowel");
else if(alpha=='i')
printf("It is vowel");
else if(alpha=='o')
printf("It is vowel");
else if(alpha=='u')
printf("It is vowel");
else
printf("It is not a vowel");
getch();
return 0;
}
```

Output:

RUN1
enter an alphabet
e
It is vowel

RUN 2
enter an alphabet
b
It is not a vowel

1.1 Switch Statement

- In the if-else statement one of the two alternatives can be selected.
- In nested if-else many alternatives can be selected but it is time consuming and complexity increases as the number of alternatives increases. The program becomes difficult to read and understand.
- Hence, to overcome the above drawbacks C has provides multi-way selection statement called switch statement. Allows the user to select any one of the several alternatives directly by the values of an expression.
- A switch statement begins with switch keyword followed by value expression in parenthesis (). These values are called case values. These case values usually are constants.
- If value in switch expression matches against the case label then the control is transferred to the particular case label and statements of that case label are executed.
- Break statement is included at the end of each block of case, signals the end of particular case and causes an exit from switch statement.
- In addition, we can also specify default case label. It is executed when the value in switch expression does not match with any of the case labels.

Syntax:

```
switch(expression)
{
case label1: statement 1;
break;
case label2: statement 2;
break;
.
.
.
```

```
default: default_statement;
}
```

2.3 Flowchart

Example programs:

1. Write a C program to illustrate switch statement for computing area of different geometrical fig.

```
#include<stdio.h>
void main()
{
int fig;
float side, base, length, breadth, height, area, radius;
printf(" 1 circle\n");
printf("2 Rectangle\n");
printf(" 3 Triangle\n");
printf(" 4 Square\n");
printf("enter the fig code");
scanf("%d",&fig);
switch(fig)
{
case 1 : printf("enter the radius\n");
         scanf("%f",&radius);
         area=3.142*radius*radius;
         printf("area of circle=%f\n",area);
         break;
case 2: printf("enter the length and breadth\n");
         scanf("%f%f",&length,&breadth);
         area=length*breadth;
         printf("area of rectangle=%f\n",area);
         break;
case 3: printf("enter the base and height\n");
         scanf("%f%f",&base,&height);
         area=0.5*base*height;
         printf("area of triangle=%f\n",area);
```

```
        break;
case 4: printf("enter the side\n");
        scanf("%f",side);
        area=side*side;
        printf("area of square=%f\n",area);
        break;
default: printf("error in fig code\n");
        break;
}
}
```

Output:

1 Circle
2 Rectangle
3 Triangle
4 Square
Enter the fig code
2
Enter the length and breadth
2 5
Area of rectangle=10

2.4 Ternary Operator ? :

It is unusual operator used to make the two-way decisions. This operator is popularly known as conditional operator. It is combination of ? and ;

Syntax:
Condtional expression ? expression 1 : expression 2;

Conditional expression is evaluated first. If it is evaluated as true or non-zero then expression 1 is executed. Otherwise, expression 2 is executed.

It is similar to simple if-else statement.

For eg.,

if(x>0)
Flag=1;
else
Flag=0;

It can be written using ternary operator as,

Flag=x>0 ? 1:0;

2.5 Iterative Statements

- Iterative means repetitive, this statement executes the segment of statements or instructions for given number of times or until the specified condition is met.
- Since the statements are executed iteratively or repetitively they are called iterative statements.
- These statements are also called looping statements.
- Execution is carried out repetitively untill condition expression is true.
- Loop exits when condition expression executes as false.
- Looping structure contains two segments, control statement and body of the loop.
- Depending upon the position ofcontrol statement, it can be classified as **entry controlled** loop and **exit controlled** loop.
- In entry controlled loop, condition is tested before exeution of the loop. If the condition is not satisfied then body of loop is not executed. These are also called as **pre-test loops**.
- In exit controlled loop, condition is tested at the end of body of loop. Body of loop is executed unconditionally for the first time. These are also called as **post-test loops**.

C language provides following looping constructs:

- The **while** loop
- The **do-while** loop
- The **for** loop

1.1.1 The While Loop:

- This is entry controlled loop.
- The loop structure is executed repetitively until the condtion is true. Once again the condtion is tested and repeated continously till the condtion becomes false.
- On evaluation of false, loop terminates and control is transferred to statements immediately following the while loop structure.
- Body of loop can contain simple or compound statements.

Syntax:

```
while(condtion)
{
Body of loop
}
```

Example program:

```
#include<stdio.h>
void main()
{
int sum=0, n=1;
        while(n<=10)
        {
        sum=sum+n;
        n=n+1;
        }
printf("sum=%d",sum);
}
```

Output:
sum=55

1.1.2 The do-while loop:

- This is exit controlled loop.
- In previous section, the condtion is tested before the execution of the loop. Body of the loop may or may not be executed at all.
- Here, body of the loop is executed atleast once first. Condition is tested at the end of loop, if condition evaluated is true it executes the loop once again otherwise, the loop is terminated.
- Control is transferred to immediately following statements on the termination of loop.

Syntax:

```
do
{
Body of loop
}while(condition)
```

Example:

```
#include<stdio.h>
#include<conio.h>
int main()
{
int num=0;
clrscr();
do
{
printf("%d\n",num++);
}
while(num<=10)
getch();
```

```
return 0;
}
```

Output:

```
0
1
2
3
4
5
6
7
8
9
10
```

1.1.3 The for loop:

- This is another entry controlled loop.
- For loop iterates for known number of times.
- It contains three parts, initialization,conditional expression and post expression

```
for(initialization; test_condtion; post_expression)
{
body of loop;
}
```

Intialization: It initializes the variable with value. This part is executed only once followed by condtional expression. variables are assigned with values using the assignment statements. These variables are called loop control variables.

Test_condition: Test condtion is the relational expression which determines when the loop should exit. If condition is true, loop is executed otherwise, loop is terminated and control is transferred to statements immediately following the loop structure.

Post_expression: Once the body of loop is executed, control is again transferred to for statement. Post_expression is used to increment or decrement a control variable controlling the loop. This process continues until the control variable fails to satisfy the test_condition.

Example:

```
#include<stdio.h>
#include<conio.h>
int main()
{
int i;
clrscr();
printf("The first ten even numbers are as follows\n");
for(i=2;i<20;i=i+2)
printf("%d\n",i);
getch();
return 0;
}
```

Output:

```
2
4
6
8
10
12
14
16
18
20
```

2.3.4 Nested for loop:

- When one for loop is placed within other for loop then it is called as **nested for loop.**
- Execution of this starts from the outer for loop and then control is passed to inner for loop.
- Inner for loop continues its execution untill its condtion is false. Once the inner for loop execution completes, the control of execution is passed to outer loop.
- Each loop must have the different index values.

Syntax:

```
for(initialization; test_condtion; post_expression)
{
        for(initialization; test_condtion; post_expression)
        {
        body of loop;
        }
}
```

Example:

```
#include<stdio.h>
#include<conio.h>
int main()
{
int x,y,sum;
clrscr();
for(x=1;x<=2;x++)
for(y=1;y<=2;y++)
        {
        Sum=x+y;
        printf("x=%d\n",x);
        printf("y=&d\n",y);
        printf("sum=%d\n",sum);
        }
getch();
```

```
return 0;
}
```

Output:

```
x=1
y=1
sum=2
x=1
y=2
sum=3
x=2
y=1
sum=3
x=2
y=3
sum=4
```

1.1.4 **Jump Statements**

- These statements are called unconditional statements.
- Jump statements transfer the control from one part of the program to another part without any condtion.
- In the situations, where we want skip the portion of loop or exit a loop these jump statements are required.
- Following are the jump statements supported by C
  - break statement
  - continue statement
  - go to statement

1.1.5 **break statement**

- This statement is used to break the loop or jump out of the loop.
- Breaking the loop is nothing but the termination of the loop.
- When break statement is used within the while, do-while, for

loop, the control comes out of the loop and continues with next the corresponding statement.

- But, if break statement is used within the switch statement it comes out of that statement, but does not come out of complete nesting.

Example:

```
#include<stido.h>
#include<conio.h>
int main()
{
int i=0;
clrscr();
while(1)
        {
        i=i+2;
        if(i>10)
        break;
        printf("%d",i);
        }
getch();
return 0;
}
```

Output:

2
4
6
8
10

1.1.6 **continue Statement:**

- In the case of break statement, it breaks the entire loop. But, continue statement breaks only the current iteration.

- Control does not come out of the loop, it just breaks current execution of loop and continue the loop with next condition. Continue statement can be considered as bypasser.

Example:

```
#include<stido.h>
#include<conio.h>
int main()
{
int i;
clrscr();
for(i=2;i<=20;i=i+2)
{
If(i==6||i==14)
{
continue;
}
printf("%d\n",i);
}
getch();
return 0;
}
```

Output:

```
2
4
8
10
12
16
18
20
```

1.1.7 **goto statement:**

- It is another type of unconditional control statement, transfers the control from one point to another point in the program.
- This statements requires the user defined labels for specifying the goto.
- Label can be placed anywhere within the program before or after the goto statement.

Syntax:
goto label;
goto is a keyword and label is the user defined symbolic constant.

- Statements immediately following the goto are skipped and control is transferred to label specified.
- goto statement may result in infinite loop so, should be careful and cautious while designing the program.
- Program can contain any number of goto statements.
- No two goto statements can have the same label

example:

```
#include<stdio.h>
void main()
{
int num=1, sum=0;
BEGIN: sum=sum+num;
        num=num+1;
        goto BEGIN;
printf("SUM=%d",sum);
}
```

Questions:

1. Write a C program to classify the triangles, equilateral, isosceles and scalene.

2. Write a C program to solve a Quadratic equation using the switch statement.

3. Write a C program to generate n Fibonacci numbers.

4. Write a C program to find the sum of N natural numbers.

5. Write the C program to find the largest of three numbers using if else statement.

6. Write a C program to reverse a given number.

7. What is the purpose of control statement in C? List various control statements in C.

8. What is the purpose of if-else statement and explain different types of if-else statements.

9. what is the purpose of switch statement.

10. what is the purpose of break statement.

11. Compare the switch statement with nested if-else statement.

12. Explain the three loop statements provided by C.

13. what is the purpose and syntax of for statement.

14. what is the purpose of nested for loop statement.

15. what is the purpose of while statement and how it differs from for statement.

Module 3:

Functions, Arrays and Strings

3. 1 Definition of a function:

A function is a procedure, or routine. In other words, the function is a group of statements, self contained block of code to perform a specific task.

Usually when certain is required to perform repeatedly, then statements required to perform intended task are also repeated. This repetition is very tedious. Hence, repetitive code is written in the form of a function and use this function. Use of functions provides modularity, easy error detection, and correction in the program.

3.2 Functions and Program Structure in C

Function is mainly used to avoid the repetition. It also provides the modularity, code manageability, code reusuability in the programs.

Inorder to use the function in the program we need three elements:

- **Function declaration:** For the functions, the declaration needs to be done before the call of the function.
- **Function definition:** It's the actual code for the function to perform certain tasks.
- **Function call:** In order to use the function in the program, we use function calls to access the function.

General Structure of function:

The function definition contains the function_name with

parameter list and the type specification of the value return by the function and function body.

```
return_data_type function_name (parameter list)
data_type_declarations_of_parameters;
{
variable declaration;
statement1;
statement2;
.
.
.
return(value);
}
```

where,

return_type represents the type of data it returns on completion of function.

function_name is the identifier name of the function.

parameter list defines the parameters/arguments that must be specified when the function is called.

Function Invocation

- Invoking function is executing code of the function of the program.
- When a program calls a function, the program control is transferred to the called function. A called function performs a defined task and when its return statement is executed or when its function-ending closing brace is reached, it returns the program control back to the main program.
- To call a function, you simply need to pass the required parameters along with the function name, and if the function returns a value, then you can store the returned value.

Arguments within the function call are referred as actual parameters and arguments in line of function definition are called formal arguments.

- For example –

```
#include <stdio.h>
/* function declaration */
int max(int num1, int num2);
int main () {
  /* local variable definition */
  int a = 100;
  int b = 200;
  int ret;

  /* calling a function to get max value */
  ret = max(a, b);

  printf( "Max value is : %d\n", ret );

  return 0;
}

/* function returning the max between two numbers */
int max(int num1, int num2) {

  /* local variable declaration */
  int result;

  if (num1 > num2)
    result = num1;
  else
    result = num2;
  return result;

}
```

3.3 Types of Functions

- The mostly commonly statements used in the program such as, printf(), scanf(), getch(), clrscr() are the functions defined in C library.

- main() is the function from where the execution of program starts.

- There are mainly two types of functions in C

- Built-in functions.

- User defined functions.

3.3.1 Built-in functions

Built in library functions are those functions which are defined by C library, example printf(), scanf(), strcat() etc. You just need to include appropriate header files to use these functions. These are already declared and defined in C libraries of C compiler by C developers. Various types of built-in library functions:

i. String manipulation functions

ii. Memory management functions

iii. Buffer management functions.

iv. Character manipulation functions.

v. Error handling functions.

i. **String manipulation functions:** Strings are often need to be manipulated by programmer according to the need of a problem. All string manipulation can be done manually by the programmer, but this makes programming complex and large. To solve this, the C supports a large number of string handling functions.

Function name	Description
strlen()	Calculates the length of string
strcpy()	Copies a string to another string
strcat()	Concatenates(joins) two strings
strcmp()	Compares two string
strlwr()	Converts string to lowercase
strupr()	Converts string to uppercase

ii. **Memory management functions:** The memory management functions are built-in library functions used to perform tasks related to memory manipulation. Various memory manipulation functions are:

- **void *calloc(int num, int size);** - This function allocates an array of **num** elements each of which size in bytes will be **size.**

- **void *calloc(int num, int size);** - This function allocates an array of num elements each of which size bytes will be size.

- **void free(void *address);** - This function releases a block of memory block specified by address.

- **void *malloc(int num);** - This function allocates an array of **num** bytes and leave them initialized.

- **void *realloc(void *address, int newsize);** - This function re-allocates memory extending it upto **newsize**.

iii. **Buffer management functions:** Buffer is temporary location shared by programs, hardware device to perform their tasks. Buffer manipulation functions in C work on the address of the memory block rather than the values inside the address.

Functions	Description
memset()	It is used to initialize a specified number of bytes to null or any other value in the buffer
memcpy()	It is used to copy a specified number of bytes from one memory to another
memmove()	It is used to copy a specified number of bytes from one memory to another or to overlap on same memory. Difference between memmove and memcpy is, overlap can happen on memmove whereas memcpy should be done in non-destructive way
memcmp()	It is used to compare specified number of characters from two buffers
memicmp()	It is used to compare specified number of characters from two buffers regardless of the case of the characters
memchr()	It is used to locate the first occurrence of the character in the specified string

iv. **Character manipulation functions:** The C language features a built in character handling functions designed to test or manipulate individual characters in C program. The functions are all defined in the ctype.h header file.

Function	Description
islower(*ch*)	check whether lowercase letter of the alphabet, *a* to *z*
isupper(*ch*)	Check whether an uppercase letter of the alphabet, *A* to *Z*
isalnum(*ch*)	check whether letter of the alphabet (upper- or lowercase) or a number

v. **Error Handling Functions:** These built in functions are used to manage the errors during C programming. Various error handling functions used in C are:

- **void perror(const char *str):** Display message on that standard error output that describes the last error encountered in a C program.

- **char *strerror(int errcode):** Returns a string describing error code passed as argument errorcode.

3.3.2 User defined functions: User-defined functions are those functions which are defined by the user at the time of writing program. Functions are made for code reusability and for saving time and space.

3.4 Argument Passing Mechanism:

Functions are invoked by their names. If the function is without argument, it can be called directly using its name. List of parameters are passed to functions that are defined with parameters. But for functions with arguments, we have two ways to call them,

- **Call by Value.**
- **Call by Reference.**

3.4.1 Call by Value:

In this invoking, we pass the values of arguments which are stored or copied into the formal parameters of functions. Hence, the changes made are not visible outside the function definition.

```
#include<stdio.h>
#include<conio.h>
int area(int length, int breadth)
{
int a;
a=length*breadth;
return a;
}
void main()
```

```
{
int l,b,result;
printf("enter the length");
scanf("%d",&l);
printf("enter the breadth");
scanf("%d",&b);
result=area(l,b);
printf("Area=%d",result);
getch();
}
```

Output:

Enter the length 5

Enter the breadth 5

Area= 25

3.4.2 Call by Reference:

In this address of the variable is passed as arguments. In this case the formal parameter can be taken as a reference or a pointer, in both the case they will change the values of the original variable. The changed value is visible outside the function.

```
#include<stdio.h>
#include<conio.h>
void swap(int *a, int *b)
{
int temp;
temp=*a;
*a=*b;
*b=temp;
}
void main()

{
```

```
int num1,num2;
printf("enter the first number");
scanf("%d",&num1);
printf("enter the second number");
scanf("%d",&num2);
swap(num1,num2);
printf("num1=%d",num1);
printf("num2=%d",num2);
getch();
}
```

3.5 Location of Functions:

- It is essential to place the function definition with regard to main program.
- There are many ways to define main program and the function
- In first case, the function is defined before calling function from the main program.
- Another way is, first specify the main program and then define the function.
- We can also define the function in a separate file and the main program in a diifernt file and compile them separately. This type is called separate compilation.
- In real world applications, the main program defined in a file s compiled and accesses the library and other user defined functions.

- The execution of the program starts from the main program. For execution of any function, we must always call from the main function.

3.6 void and Parameter Less Functions:

3.6.1 void function

- A void function is a function that does not return any value.
- A void function is created similar to the function that returns a value.
- But, the return type used is void, which indicates that it does not return any value.
- In this type, it performs the specific task and control is transferred to calling function.

  syntax: void function_name(int a, int b);

  where,

  void is return type.

  function_name is the name of the function.

  a and b are integer type variables passed as parameters to the function.

- **return** keyword is specified to return back to calling function before ending the void function.

3.6.2 Parameter less function

- A parameter less function is a function that does not have any parameters.
- In this void keyword is used twice, one at the beginning of

function declaration and inside the parenthesis to indicate there are no parameters.

- Even we can leave mentioning void inside parenthesis, but still it works same.

- **Syntax: void function_name(void);**

3.7 Recursion:

Recursion is a special nesting functions, where a function calls itself inside it. We must have certain condition to break out of the recursion, otherwise recursion is infinite. This process of repetition is called as recursion.

example:

```
#include<stdio.h>
#include<conio.h>
int factorial(int x);
void main()
{
 int a,b;
 clrscr();
 printf("Enter no.");
 scanf("%d",&a);
 b=factorial(a);
 printf("%d",b);
 getch();
}
int factorial(int x)
{
 int r=1;
 if(x==1) return 1;
 else r=x*factorial(x-1);
 return r;
}
```

Arrays

- An array is the collection of elements of the same data type stored in consecutive memory location. It can be defined as an ordered list of homogeneous data elements.
- It can be used to store the values of different data types such as int, float, char or double.
- An array is referenced or described by a single name or identifier.
- Each value in the array is referenced by a single name which name of the array or subscript or index enclosed in a pair of square brackets.
- Subscript indicates the position of the individual data item in the array. Individual data items are called elements of the array.
- This subscript should be unsigned integer and as subscripts are used sometimes array are called as subscripted variables.

The General structure of an array containing n-elements:

array[0]	array[1]	array[2]	....	array[n-1]

where,

0,1,2. . . . n-1 are subscripts

array[0] represents the first element in an array

array[1] represents the second element in an array

array[2] represents the third element in an array

.

.

array[n1] represents the nth element in an array

In general we can say, for array[i] indicates the i-1th element of array. Here size of array is **0 to n-1**.

3.8 Types of Arrays

Arrays can be classified into three different types,

1. One-dimensional array.
2. Two-dimensional array.
3. Three-dimensional or multi-dimensional array.

1. One-dimensional array:

- An array which contains only one subscript is called a one-dimensional array.
- It is similar to row or column matrix and used to perform either row or column operation.
- It is used to store the linear list of values of the same data type.
- All these data items are accessed using the same name and single subscript.
- Elements in one-dimensional array can be stored in the index values starting from zero to n-1th position.

1.1 Declaration of a One-Dimensional Array

A One-dimensional array can be declared using the following syntax,

data_type array_name [size];

where,

data_type is any basic data type or user defined data type.

array_name represents the name of an array.

size represents the number of elements or values to be stored. The size must be an integer constant specified within the pair of square brackets.

Example:

int list[10];

char name[20];

float abc[10];

double x[100];

Write a program to accept the values of an array A of size n and print the same array as output. (Read array A of n size and print the same)

```
#include<stdio.h>
#include<conio.h>
void main()
{
int a[10], n,i;
clrscr();
printf("enter the size of an array\n");
scanf("%d",&n);
printf("\n enter the values of an array\n");
for(i=0;i<n;i++)
scanf("%d",&a[i]);
printf("\n the values of array are\n");
for(i=0;i<n;i++)
printf("a[%d]=%d",i,a[i]);
getch();
}
```

Output:

enter the size of an array

5

enter the values of an array

1 2 3 4 5

the values of array are

1 2 3 4 5

Write a program to read the array elements of A and B of size n and perform the addition operation for an array C and print the output.

```
#include<stdio.h>
#include<conio.h>
void main()
{
int a[10], b[10], c[10], i, n;
clrscr();
printf("enter the size of array n\n");
scanf("%d",&n);
printf("\nenter the elements of array A\n");
for(i=0;i<n;i++)
scanf("%d",&a[i]);
printf("\n enter the elements of array B\n");
for(i=0;i<n;i++)
scanf("%d",&b[i]);
printf("Process of two arrays\n");
for(i=0;i<n;i++)
{
c[i]=a[i]+b[i];
}
printf("The resultant matrix is \n");
for(i=0;i<n;i++)
printf("c[%d]=%d",i,c[i]);
```

```
getch();
}
```

Output:

```
enter the size of array n
2
enter the elements of array A
1 2
enter the elements of array B
3 4
Process of two arrays
The resultant matrix is
c[0]=4
c[1]=6
```

Write a program to sort the array elements in ascending order using the bubble sort.

```
#include<stdio.h>
#include<conio.h>
void main()
{
int a[10], n,i, j, temp;
clrscr();
printf("enter the size of an array\n");
scanf("%d",&n);
printf("\n enter the elements of an array\n");
for(i=0;i<n;i++)
scanf("%d",&a[i]);
for(i=0;i<n-1;i++)
{
for(j=n-1;j>i;j--)
{
if(a[j]<a[j-1])
{
temp=a[j];
```

```
a[j]=a[j-1];
a[j-1]=temp;
}
}
}
printf("\n The elements of an sorted array are\n");
for(i=0;i<n;i++)
printf(" %d",a[i]);
getch();
}
```

Output:

```
enter the size of an array
5
enter the elements of an array
2 1 6 5 4
The elements of an sorted array are
1 2 4 5 6
```

Write a program to read the array elements from keyboard and find the sum and average of n elements.

```
#include<stdio.h>
#include<conio.h>
void main()
{
int a[10], n, I;
float sum=0, avg;
clrscr();
printf("enter the size of an array n\n");
scanf("%d",&n);
printf("\n enter the elements of an array\n");
for(i=0;i<n;i++)
scanf("%d",&a[i]);
for(i=0;i<n;i++)
```

```
{
sum=sum+a[i];
}
printf("sum=%d",sum);
avg=sum/n;
printf("average=%d",avg);
getch();
}
```

Write a program to evaluate polynomial $f(x)=a_4x^4+a_3x^3+a_2x^2+a_1x^1+a_0$ from the given value of x and its co-efficients using Honer's method.

```
#include<stdio.h>
#include<conio.h>
void main()
{
int a[10], i, x, P;
clrscr();
printf("enter the 5 co-efficients \n");
for(i=0;i<=4;i++)
scanf("%d",&a[i]);
printf("enter the value of x\n");
scanf("%d",&x);
P=a[4];
for(i=3;i>=0;i--)
{
P=P*x+a[i];
}
printf("polynomial=%d",P);
getch();
}
```

Output:

Note:

Amount of memory that can be allocated can be computed as,

Total Size=size*[sizeof(data_type)];

where,

size is the number of elements in array.

sizeof( ) is an unary operator to find the size in bytes.

data_type is basic data type or user defined data type.

1.2 Initialization of one-dimensional array

Initialization is the process of assigning the value to variable. Similar to initialization of the ordinary variable, elements of an array can be initialized individually one by one in the same way. You can also initialize the values of an array during the time of declaration.

The syntax used to initialize one-dimensional array is,

data_type array_name[size]={'v1', 'v2', ... 'vn'}

where,

data_type is the basic data_type or user defined data type which is used to represent.

array_name represents the name of an array

size represents the maximum number of elements in the array.

{'v1', 'v2', ... 'vn' } are intial values of an array that are initialized enclosed within pair of curly braces. The elements are separated by comma and written in the order they are assigned.

Example:

int list[5]={1, 2, 3, 4, 5};

float abc[5]={1.5, 2.5, 3.5, 4.5, 5.5};

Write a program to initialize the elements of an array and print the same as output.

```
#include<stdio.h>
#include<conio.h>
void main()
{
int a[10]={1, 2, 3, 4, 5}, i;
clrscr();
printf(" The elements of an array are\n");
for(i=0;i<5;i++)
printf("%d",a[i]);
getch();
}
```

Output:

The elements of an array are

1 2 3 4 5

Write a program to initialize the array elements of A and B and find the sum of two matrices.

```
#include<stdio.h>
#include<conio.h>
void main()
{
int a[10]={1, 2, 3, 4, 5}, b[10]={1, 2, 3, 4, 5}, c[5], i;
clrscr();
for(i=0;i<5;i++)
{
c[i]=a[i]+b[i];
}
printf(" The sum of elements of an array are\n");
for(i=0;i<5;i++)
printf(" c[%d]=%d \n",i, c[i]);
getch();
```

```
}
```

Output:

The sum of elements of an array are

c[0]=2

c[1]=4

c[2]=6

c[3]=8

c[4]=10

Write a program to initialize the array elements of A and B and find the subtraction of two matrices.

```
#include<stdio.h>
#include<conio.h>
void main()
{
int a[10]={2, 4, 6, 8, 10}, b[10]={1, 2, 3, 4, 5}, c[5], i;
clrscr();
printf("Subtraction of two matrices\n");
for(i-0;i<5;i++)
{
c[i]=a[i]-b[i];
}
printf(" The resultant matrix is\n");
for(i=0;i<5;i++)
printf(" c[%d]=%d \n",i, c[i]);
getch();
}
```

Output:

The sum of elements of an array are

c[0]=1

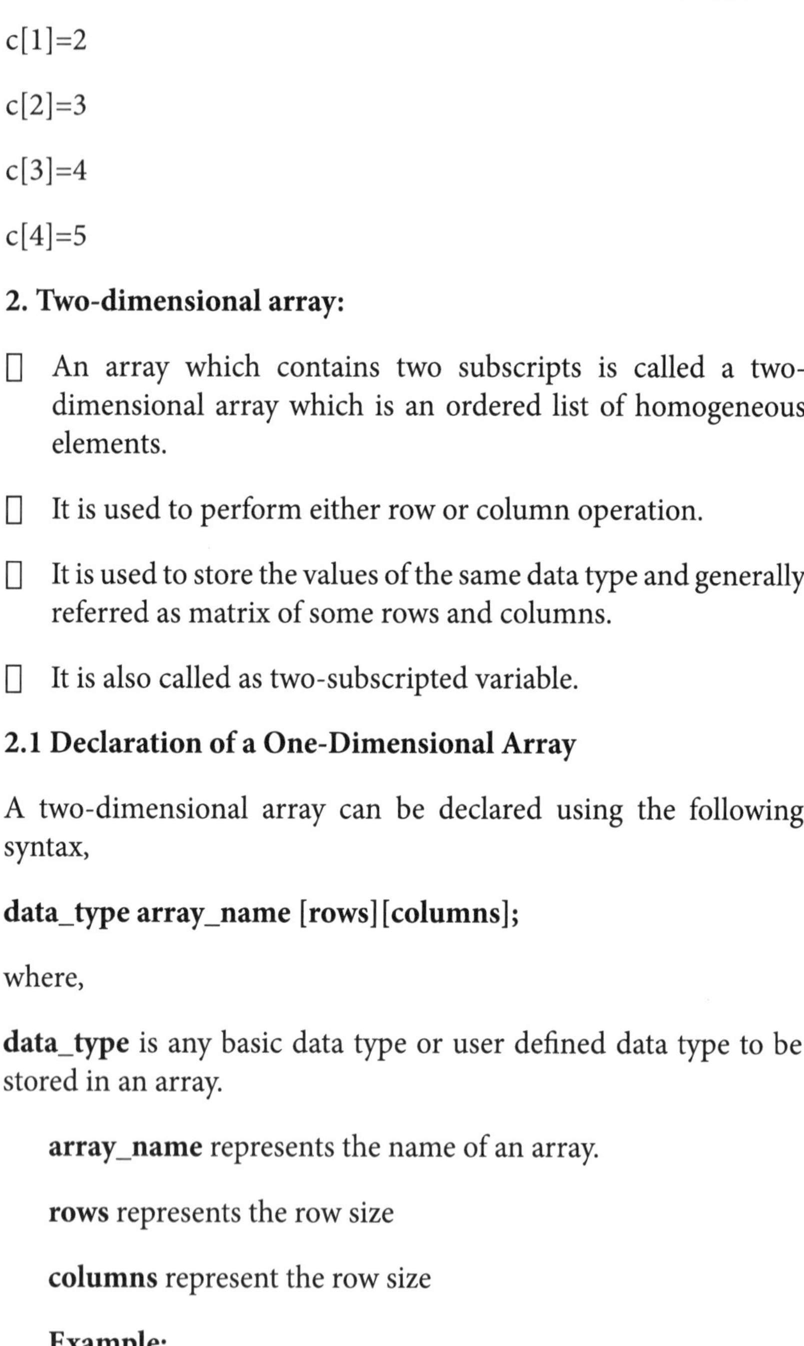

c[1]=2

c[2]=3

c[3]=4

c[4]=5

2. Two-dimensional array:

- An array which contains two subscripts is called a two-dimensional array which is an ordered list of homogeneous elements.
- It is used to perform either row or column operation.
- It is used to store the values of the same data type and generally referred as matrix of some rows and columns.
- It is also called as two-subscripted variable.

2.1 Declaration of a One-Dimensional Array

A two-dimensional array can be declared using the following syntax,

data_type array_name [rows][columns];

where,

data_type is any basic data type or user defined data type to be stored in an array.

array_name represents the name of an array.

rows represents the row size

columns represent the row size

Example:

```
int list[10][10];

char name[20][20];

float abc[10][10];

double x[10][10];
```

Write a program to accept the elements of an array A of size mxn and print the same array as output.

```
#include<stdio.h>
#include<conio.h>
void main()
{
int a[10][10],m, n,i, j;
clrscr();
printf("enter the size of an array m  & n\n");
scanf("%d%d",&m,&n);
printf("\n enter the elements of an array\n");
for(i=0;i<m;i++)
for(j=0;j<n;j++)
scanf("%d",&a[i][j]);
printf("\n the resultant matrix is \n");
for(i=0;i<n;i++)
for(j=0;j<n;j++)
printf("a[%d][%d]=%d ",i, j, a[i][j]);
getch();
}
```

Output:

enter the size of an array m & n

2 2

enter the elements of an array

1 2 3 4

the resultant matrix is

1 2 3 4

Write a program to read the array elements of A and B of size m and n and perform the addition operation for an array C and print the output.

```
#include<stdio.h>
#include<conio.h>
void main()
{
int a[10][10], b[10][10], c[10][10], i, j, m, n;
clrscr();
printf("enter the size of array m and n\n");
scanf("%d%d",&m,&n);
printf("\nenter the elements of array A\n");
for(i=0;i<m;i++)
for(j=0;j<n;j++)
scanf("%d",&a[i][j]);
printf("\n enter the elements of array B\n");
for(i=0;i<m;i++)
for(j=0;j<n;j++)
scanf("%d",&b[i][j]);
for(i=0;i<m;i++)
{
for(j=0;j<n;j++)
{
c[i][j]=a[i][j]+b[i][j];
}
}
printf("The resultant matrix C is \n");
for(i=0;i<m;i++)
for(j=0;j<n;j++)
printf("c[%d][%d]=%d",i, j, c[i][j]);
```

```
getch();
}
```

Output:

```
enter the size of array n
2 2
enter the elements of array A
1 2 3 4
enter the elements of array B
1 2 3 4
The resultant matrix is
c[0][0]=2
c[0][1]=4
c[1][0]=6
c[1][1]=8
```

Write a program to read the array elements of A of size m and n and B of size p and q. Perform the subtraction operation for an array C and print the output.

```
#include<stdio.h>
#include<conio.h>
void main()
{
int a[10][10], b[10][10], c[10][10], i, j, m, n, p, q;
clrscr();
printf("enter the size of array m and n\n");
scanf("%d%d",&m,&n);
printf("enter the size of array p and q\n");
scanf("%d%d",&p,&q);
printf("\nenter the elements of array A(mxn)\n");
for(i=0;i<m;i++)
for(j=0;j<n;j++)
scanf("%d",&a[i][j]);
printf("\n enter the elements of array B(pxq)\n");
for(i=0;i<p;i++)
```

```
for(j=0;j<q;j++)
scanf("%d",&b[i][j]);
for(i=0;i<m;i++)
{
for(j=0;j<p;j++)
{
c[i][j]=a[i][j]-b[i][j];
}
}
printf("The resultant matrix A is \n");
for(i=0;i<m;i++)
for(j=0;j<n;j++)
printf("a[%d][%d]=%d",i, j, a[i][j]);
printf("The resultant matrix A is \n");
for(i=0;i<m;i++)
for(j=0;j<n;j++)
printf("a[%d][%d]=%d \n",i, j, a[i][j]);
printf("The resultant matrix B is \n");
for(i=0;i<p;i++)
for(j=0;j<q;j++)
printf("b[%d][%d]=%d\n ",i, j, b[i][j]);
printf("The resultant matrix C is \n");
for(i=0;i<m;i++)
for(j=0;j<p;j++)
printf("c[%d][%d]=%d\n ",i, j, c[i][j]);
getch();
}
```

Output:

```
enter the size of array m and n
2 2
enter the size of array p and q
2 2
enter the elements of array A
1 2 3 4
```

enter the elements of array B
1 2 3 4
The resultant matrix A is
a[0][0]=1
a[0][1]=2
a[1][0]=3
a[1][1]=4
The resultant matrix B is
b[0][0]=1
b[0][1]=2
b[1][0]=3
b[1][1]=4
The resultant matrix C is
c[0][0]=0
c[0][1]=0
c[1][0]=0
c[1][1]=0

2.2 Initialization of two-dimensional array

The elements of two-dimensional array can be initialized either one at a time or all at once.

The syntax used to initialize two-dimensional array is,

data_type array_name[size1][size2]={'v1', 'v2', ... 'vn'}

where,

data_type is the basic data_type or user defined data type which is used to represent.

array_name represents the name of an array

size1 and size2 represents the maximum number of rows and columns in the array.

{'v1', 'v2', ... 'vn' } are intial values of an array that are initialized enclosed within pair of curly braces. The elements are separated by comma and written in the order they are assigned.

Example:

int list[3][3]={1, 2, 3, 4, 5, 6, 7, 8, 9};

The above example can also be represented as,

list[0][0]=1 list[0][1]=2 list[0][2]=3

list[1][0]=4 list[1][1]=5 list[1][2]=6

list[2][0]=7 list[2][1]=8 list[2][2]=9

Write a program to initialize the elements of an array and print the same as output.

```
#include<stdio.h>
#include<conio.h>
void main()
{
int a[2][2]={1, 2, 3, 4}, i, j;
clrscr();
printf(" The elements of an array A are\n");
for(i=0;i<2;i++)
for(j=0;j<2;j++)
printf("%d ",a[i][j]);
getch();
}
```

Output: The elements of an array are

1 2 3 4

3. Multidimensional array:

If the array contains more than two subscripts, then it is called as multi-dimensional array. Dimensionality of the determined by the number of pairs of square brackets placed after the array name. As the number of subscript increases, it increases the complexity of the program.

3.1 Declaration of a multi-Dimensional Array

A multidimensional array can be declared using the following syntax,

data_type array_name [size1][size2] [size3];

where,

data_type is any basic data type or user defined data type to be stored in an array.

array_name represents the name of an array.

size1 represents the number of rows

size2 represent the number of columns

size3 represent the number of pages

Example:

int list[10][10[10];

Strings

3.9 Definition of String

A string is a one-dimensional array of characters which is terminated by a null character. The size of the string always starts with 0 and ends with n+1.

Let us consider the example to show how the string is stored in the main memory of the computer.

Index 0 1 2 3 4 5

H	E	L	L	O	\0

Here, the first element of the string is stored in 1st position, the second element in 2nd position and so on. The last element of the string always gets terminated by a null character (\0) which is in n+1 position.

3.10 Declaration and initialization of String

A character array or a string is declared as,

char variable_name[size];

where,

char represents the data type which is used to store the array of characters.

variable_name represents the name of a string.

size represents the size of a string.

Example:

char a[10];

A character array or string variable is initialized by either assigning a charcter constant individually or assigning all the characters at a time.

- When you initialize the string variable by assigning character individually we use single quotes ' '.

Example:

char array[10]={'H','E','L','L','O','\0'};

- In the above example, note that whenever we initialize the character constants individually we have to represent null characters (\0) manually by the programmer (user).

- When you initialize string characters collectively together, we use double quotes.

Example:

char array[8]={ "HELLO" };

In this example, the null character will be initialized automatically by the system at the end of the string.

3.11 Reading and Writing Strings

A string can be read or written out using the input/output statements.Some of the input and output operations of the string are as follows:

i. printf( ) and scanf( ) statements.

ii. gets( ) and puts( ) statements.

iii. getchar( ) and putchar( ) statements.

i. printf( ) and scanf( ) statements.

- The printf( ) and scanf( ) statcments are the functions which are used to perform input and output operations
- The scanf( ) statement is the function which reads the character from the keyboard and stores them in the variables according to the specified format.
- When we want to read the string we need to use the **%s** format specifier in scanf( ) statement.

  example:

  scanf("%s",name);

  The above example indicate that we are reading the name.

- The printf( ) statement function along with %s format specifier prints a string stored in the character array variable. We can use this function to display string data in two ways

  - You can pass string data directly in the printf( ) statement.

    example: printf("Hello, Welcome to RYMEC\n");

  - You can store the string data in character array and pass the array as parameter to printf( ) function.

    example: char str[10]={ "Hello, Welcome to C \n"};

    printf("%s",str);

- Here the major disadvantage is that scanf( ) and printf( ) statements can read the characters until the space or newline characters is encountered.

Read the string from keyboard and print the output of the same input string.

```
#include<stdio.h>
#include<conio.h>
#include<string.h>
void main()
{
char str[10];
printf("enter the string\n");
scanf("%s",str);
printf("\nString is %s", str);
getch();
}
```

Output:

```
enter the string
RYMEC
String is RYMEC
```

Displaying the specific days of a week using printf statement.

```
#include<stdio.h>
#include<conio.h>
#include<string.h>
void main()
{
char str1[10]={"Monday"};
char str2[10]={'s', 'u' 'n', 'd', 'a', 'y', '\0'};
clrscr();
printf("str1=%s",str1);
printf("\nstr2=%s",str2);
getch();
}
```

Output:

```
str1=Monday
str2=Sunday
```

ii. gets( ) and puts( ) statements.

- The **gets( )** function reads the string from keyboard and it is similar to scanf( ) statement function.
- But, the major difference between the gets( ) and scanf( ) statement is that gets( ) function can read the whole sentence which is combination of multiple characters along with white space as a character.
- While in scanf( ) statement it can read the character until the white space is encountered in the sentence.
- This gets( ) function is also called as an **unformatted input statement**.
- The **puts( )** statement function prints the characters or string which is stored in the string variable. The puts( ) function is

similar to that of printf( ) function.

- The puts( ) function is also called as an **unformatted output statement**.

Example:

Write a program to accept the string from the keyboard and print the same as output using puts( ) and gets( ) function.

```
#include<stdio.h>
#include<conio.h>
#include<string.h>
void main()
{
char str[10];
printf("enter the string\n");
gets(str);
printf("\nThe output string is ");
puts(str);
getch();
}
```

Output:

```
enter the string
RYMEC
The output string is RYMEC
```

iii. getchar( ) and putchar( ) statements.

- The **putchar( )** function writes the character to the standard output device ie., monitor.
- This function operates with only one character at a time.
- The syntax used is,

  putchar(variable_name);

- The **getchar( )** function reads the character from the standard input device ie., keyboard.
- This function helps us to input the one character at a time.
- The syntax used is,

  getchar(variable_name);

Write a program to accept the array of string from the array of string from the keyboard and display the same as output using putchar( ) and getchar( ) function.

```
#include<stdio.h>
#include<conio.h>
#include<string.h>
void main()
{
char ch;
clrscr();
printf("enter the word\n");
getchar(ch);
printf("\nThe output string is  ");
putchar(ch);
getch();
}
```

Output:
enter the string
RYMEC
The output string is RYMEC

3.12 String Manipulation Functions

Some of the common and useful string handling or manipulation functions are discussed below:

3.12.1 strlen( ) function:

- The strlen( ) function is used to find the length of the string.
- The syntax is ,

strlen(string);

- It takes string as the parameter and count the number of characters in the string.

Example:

```
#include<stdio.h>
#include<conio.h>
#include<string.h>
void main()
{
char str[10]={"RYMEC"};
int result;
result=strlen(str);
printf("String length=%d",result);
getch();
}
```

Output:

String length=5

3.12.2 strcmp( ) function:

- The strcmp( ) function is used to compare two strings data.
- The syntax that is used here is,

strcmp(string1,string2);

- Here, strcmp( ) function takes two parameters of strings for comparision.
- The returned value can be **zero** or **greater than zero** or **less than zero**.

- A **zero** value indicates that both the strings are equal.
- A value which is **greater than zero** indicates that the first character of string1is greater than string2 and does not match with string2.

- A value which is **less than zero** indicates the first character of string1 is less than that of string2 and does not match with string2.

Example:

```
#include<stdio.h>
#include<conio.h>
#include<string.h>
void main()
{
char str1[10], str2[10];
clrscr();
printf("enter the string1\n");
gets(str1);
printf("\n enter the string2\n");
gets(str2);
if(strcmp(str1,str2)==0)
{
printf("\n Both strings are equal  ");
}
else
printf("\n Both strings are not equal  ");
getch();
}
```

Output:

```
enter the string1
RYMEC
enter the string2
college
Both strings are not equal
```

3.12.3 strncmp( ) function:

- The strcmp( ) function is used to compare two strings data upto a specified number of characters.
- The syntax that is used here is,

strcnmp(string1, string2, n);

- Here, strcmp( ) function takes three parameters where two parameters are the strings which we have to be compared and third parameter is number of characters upto which the two strings are compared..

Example:

```
#include<stdio.h>
#include<conio.h>
#include<string.h>
void main()
{
char str1[10]={"RYMEC"}, str2[10]={"college"};
int n=2;
clrscr();
if(strncmp(str1,str2,n)==0)
{
printf("\n Both strings are equal ");
}
else
printf("\n Both strings are not equal ");
getch();
}
```

Output:

Both strings are not equal

3.12.4 strcat( ) function:

- The strcat( ) function is used to concatenate the two strings together. ie., the values of string2 is added to string1. The syntax that is used here is,

strcat(string1, string2);

- Here, strcat( ) function takes two parameters to add second string to first string. Second sting is appended to first string and concatenated string is stored in the first string.

Example:

```
#include<stdio.h>
#include<conio.h>
#include<string.h>
void main()
{
char str1[10], str2[10];
clrscr();
printf("enter the string1\n");
gets(str1);
printf("\n enter the string2\n");
gets(str2);
strcat(str1,str2);
puts(str1);
strcat(str2,str1);
puts(str2);
getch();
}
```

Output:

```
enter the string1
RYMEC
enter the string2
 college
RYMEC college
college RYMEC
```

3.12.5 strncat( ) function:

- The strcat( ) function is used to concatenate the two strings together epending upon the number of characters that the user specified.

- The syntax that is used here is,
  strncat(string1, string2, n);

- Here, strcat( ) function takes two parameters to add second string to first string. Second sting is appended to first string and concatenated string is stored in the first string.

Example:

```
#include<stdio.h>
#include<conio.h>
#include<string.h>
void main()
{
char str1[10], str2[10], result;
clrscr();
printf("enter the string1\n");
gets(str1);
printf("\n enter the string2\n");
gets(str2);
printf("\n enter the value of n\n");
scanf("%d",n);
result=strncat(str1,str2,n);
puts(str1);
getch();
}
```

Output:

```
enter the string1
RYMEC
enter the string2
 college
enter the value of n
3
RYMECcol
```

3.12.6 strcpy( ) function:

- The strcpy( ) function is used to copy the content of string2 to the content of string1.
- The syntax that is used here is,
  strcpy(string1, string2);

- Here, strcpy( ) function takes two parameters and it copies the contents of string2 to the sring1.

Example:

```
#include<stdio.h>
#include<conio.h>
#include<string.h>
void main()
{
char str1[10], str2[10], result;
clrscr();
printf("enter the string1\n");
gets(str1);
printf("\n enter the string2\n");
gets(str2);
result=strcpy(str1,str2);
gets(result);
getch();
}
```

Output:

```
enter the string1
RYMEC
enter the string2
 college
college
```

3.12.7 strchr( ) function:

- The strchr( ) function is used to search a specific character in the string.

- The syntax that is used here is,
 strchr(string1, character);

```
#include<stdio.h>
#include<conio.h>
#include<string.h>
void main()
{
char str[10], ch, result;
clrscr();
printf("enter the string\n");
gets(str);
printf("\n enter the character to be searched\n");
scanf("%c",&ch);
result=strchr(str,ch);
printf("result=%c",result);
getch();
}
```

Output:

3.12.8 strlwr( ) function:

- The strlwr( ) function is used to convert the characters stored in a string into the lower case.
- The syntax that is used here is,
 strlwr(string);
- Here, it takes one parameter string and returns the resultant string by converting all th characters to lower case.

```
#include<stdio.h>
#include<conio.h>
#include<string.h>
void main()
{
char str[10]={"HELLO"};
clrscr();
```

```
printf("String in lower case : %s", strlwr(str));
getch();
}
```

Output:

String in lower case : hello

3.12.9 strrev( ) function:

- The strrev( ) function is used to reverse the string.
- The syntax that is used here is,

    strupr(string);
- Here, it takes one parameter string and returns the resultant string by reversing the order of all the characters.

```
#include<stdio.h>
#include<conio.h>
#include<string.h>
void main()
{
char str[10]={"hello"};
clrscr();
printf("Reverse string is : %s", strrev(str));
getch();
}
```

Output:

Reverse string is : olleh

Questions:

1. What is function? What is its purpose.
2. Explain three elements of a function.
3. What is purpose of function declaration? How is it written.
4. What do you mean by actual and formal parameters?
5. Explain two methods of passing arguments to a function.
6. What is recursion? Explain with an example.
7. Explain the general structure of array.
8. What is an array? How do you classify arrays?
9. Explain array declaration.
10. What is array initialization. State various ways of array initialization.
11. How multidimensional arrays defined. Show the structure of two dimensional array.
12. What is string? How it is declared and initialized.
13. Explain the string handling functions defined for strings.
14. Write C program to compare two strings.
15. Write C program to calculate length of the string.
16. Write a C program to perform following matrix operation.
    - Transpose of a matrix
    - Inverse of a matrix.
    - Interchange of two rows or columns.

Module 4:

Structures and file management

4.1 Definition of a structure

A structure is a user defined data type, which is used to store values of different data types together under the same structure name.

4.2 How to define the structure in the program

- You must define the structure before using it in a program.
- Definition of structure always starts with the **struct** keyword followed by the **name of the structure** (structure name), a pair of curly braces containing declaration of set of variables called **structure members** and then **semicolon.**
- The syntax of structure definition is as follows:

```
struct structure_name
{
data_type1 variablc 1;
data_type1 variable2;
.
.
data_typen variable;
};
```

Example:

```
struct student
{
int rollno;
char name[20];
```

```
int marks;
char grade;
};
```

4.3 Declaring structure variable:

After defining the structure, you can declare the variables of the structure type in the same way as you declare variables of predefined datatype.
The syntax for declaring the structure variable is as follows:

struct structure_name varaiblename;
example:

struct student s1;

- You can also declare multiple structure variable in the single line.

- The syntax is

  struct structure_name var1, var2, var3......varn;

  eg., struct student s1,s2,s3,s4,s5;

- By combining the definition of structure and structure variable, the syntax is as follows

  struct structure_name
  {
  data_type1 variable 1;
  data_type1 variable2;
  .
  .
  data_typen variable;
  } structure var1, structure var2, ...structure varn;
  example:
  struct student

```
{
int rollno;
char name[20];
int marks;
char grade[2];
} stud1, stud2, stud3, stud4, stud5;
```

4.4 Initialization of structure variable:

- Initializing the structure variable involves assigning the values to the structure members. You can assign the values to the structure members all at a time or one at a time.
- Here, we have two approaches in initialization of structure variables. They are

i. In the first approach, the declaration of the structure variable and initialization of structure members are done using a single line code.
   For eg., struct student student1={“101”,”James”};

ii. In the second approach, we need to declare the structure variable first then initialize the structure variable one after the other. The syntax that we use to initialize is as follows:

structure_varaible_name . structure_member=value;

example:

```
struct student student1;
student1.rollno=101;
student1.age=25;
student1.name=”James”;
student1.college=”RYMEC”;
```

Write a program to accept name,rollno, age, and college of the student and print the same using structure initialization.

```
#includc<stdio.h>
#include<conio.h>
```

```
#include<string.h>
void main()
{
struct student
{
char name[20];
int rollno;
int age;
char college[20];
};
struct student s1;
s1.name="Shiva";
s1.rollno=20;
s1.age=25;
s1.college="RYMEC Ballari";
printf("student details are as follows\n");
printf("name=%s\n",s1.name);
printf("rollno=%d\n",s1.rollno);
printf("age=%d\n",s1.age);
printf("college=%s\n",s1.college);
getch();
}
```

Output:

```
name=Shiva
rollno=20
age=25
college=RYMEC Ballari
```

Write a program to accept name, rollno, age, and college of the student and print the same using structure declaration.

```
#include<stdio.h>
#include<conio.h>
#include<string.h>
```

```
void main()
{
struct student
{
char name[20];
int rollno;
int age;
char college[20];
};
struct student s1;
printf("enter the rollno of student1 \n");
scanf("%d",&s1.rollno);
printf("enter the name of student1 \n");
scanf("%s",&s1.name);
printf("enter the age of student1 \n");
scanf("%d",&s1.age);
printf("enter the college name of student1 \n");
scanf("%s",&s1.college);
printf("student details are as follows\n");
printf("name=%s\n",s1.name);
printf("rollno=%d\n",s1.rollno);
printf("age=%d\n",s1.age);
printf("college=%s\n",s1.college);
getch();
}
```

Output:

```
enter the rollno of student1
01
enter the name of student1
Shiva
enter the age of student1
25
enter the college name of student1
RYMEC
```

```
student details are as follows
rollno=01
name=Shiva
age=25
college=RYMEC
```

Write a program to accept name nd age of 3 employees and print the same using structure declaration.

```
#include<stdio.h>
#include<conio.h>
#include<string.h>
void main()
{
struct employee
{
char name[20];
int age;
};
struct employee emp1, emp2, emp3;
printf("enter the details of employee1 \n");
printf("enter the name of the employee1 \n");
scanf("%s",&emp1.name);
printf("enter the age of employee1 \n");
scanf("%d",&emp1.age);
printf("enter the name of the employee2 \n");
scanf("%s",&emp2.name);
printf("enter the age of employee2 \n");
scanf("%d",&emp2.age);
printf("enter the name of the employee3 \n");
scanf("%s",&emp3.name);
printf("enter the age of employee3 \n");
scanf("%d",&emp3.age);
printf("Details of the employee1  \n");
printf("name=%s\n",emp1.name);
printf("age=%d\n",emp1.age);
```

```
printf("Details of the employee2 \n");
printf("name=%s\n",emp2.name);
printf("age=%d\n",emp2.age);
getch();
}
```

Output:

```
enter the details of employee1
enter the name of the employee1
Shiva
enter the age of employee1
29
enter the name of the employee2
Prasad
enter the age of employee2
30
enter the name of the employee3
kalmutt
enter the age of employee3
30
Details of the employee1
name=Shiva
age=29
Dctails of the employee2
name=prasad
age=30
Details of the employee3
name=kalmutt
age=30
```

4.5 Structure and Arrays

Array of structure type are required in situations when you need to apply the same structure to the set of objects.

For eg.,

You need to store record of 50 students of a class where each student record has three fields ie., rollno, name, and marks. In this case, you can first define the structure containing three fields as mentioned above to represent the student record and then create an array of structure type.

Arrays of structure type in a program

```
#include<stdio.h>
#include<conio.h>
#include<string.h>
void main()
{
struct student
{
int rollno;
char name[20];
int marks;
};
struct student s[20];
int i,n;
clrscr();
printf("enter the size of an array\n");
scanf("%d",&n);
for(i=0;i<n;i++)
{
printf("enter the rollno of the student\n");
scanf("%d",&s[i].rollno);
printf("enter the name of student \n");
scanf("%s",&s[i].name);
printf("enter the marks of student \n");
scanf("%d",&s[i].marks);
}
printf("student details are ");
for(i=0;i<n;i++)
{
printf("rollno of student %d=%d\n",i+1,s[i].rollno);
```

```
printf("name of student %d=%d\n",i+1,s[i].name);
printf("marks of student %d=%d\n",i+1,s[i].marks);
}
getch();
}
```

Output:

enter the size of an array 2
enter the rollno of the student
01
enter the name of student
Shiva
enter the marks of student
55
enter the rollno of the student
02
enter the name of student
Prasad
enter the marks of student
65
student details are
rollno of student 1=01
name of student 1=Shiva
marks of student 1=55
rollno of student 2=02
name of student 2=Prasad
marks of student 1=65

4.6 Nested Structures

- You can nest (combine) a structure inside another structure.
- Structure can be nested into two different ways

  i. The first approach is the complete definition of structure is placed inside the definition of another structure.

  eg.,

  ```
  struct student
  ```

```
{
int rollno;
char name[20];
        struct date{
        int day;
        int month;
        int year;
        } dob;
} student1;
```

ii. In the second approach, the structures are defined separately and the variables of structure type is defined inside the definition of another structure.

eg.,

```
struct date
{
int date;
int month;
int year;
};
struct student
{
int rollno;
char name[20];
struct date dob;
}student1;
```

Write a program to input rollno, name, and date of birth of the student and print the same using nested structure.

```
#include<stdio.h>
#include<conio.h>
#include<string.h>
void main()
{
```

```
struct student
{
int rollno;
char name[20];
struct date
{
        int date;
        int month;
        int year;
        };
} student1;
clrscr();
printf("enter the rollno of the student1\n");
scanf("%d",&student1.rollno);
printf("enter the name of student1 \n");
scanf("%s",&student1.name);
printf("enter the date of the student \n");
scanf("%d",&student1.dob.date);
printf("enter the month of the  student \n");
scanf("%d",&student1.dob.month);
printf("enter the year of the  student \n");
printf("Output of student1 is ");
printf("rollno=%d\n",student1.rollno);
printf("name=%s\n",student1.name);
printf("date=%d\n",student1.dob.date);
printf("month=%d\n",student1.dob.month);
printf("year=%d\n",student1.dob.year);
getch();
}
```

Output:

```
enter the rollno of student1
01
enter the name of student1
Shiva
```

enter the date of the student1
30
enter the month of the student
10
enter the year of the student
1984
Output of student1 is
rollno=01
name=Shiva
date=30
month=10
year=1984

4.7 Structures with Functions

- In C language, you can pass the entire structure as parameter and return a value as a structure.
- Structures are passed by value and enable the function to alter the parameter you must pass a pointer to a structure.

- **example:**

```
#include<stdio.h>
#include<conio.h>
#include<stdlib.h>
typedef struct student
{
int rollno;
char name[20];
float marks;
}
student s1;
void print(student s1);
void main()
{
```

```
char ans;
clrscr();
do
{
printf("enter the student details");
printf("enter the rollno \n");
scanf("%d",&s1.rollno);
printf("enter the name \n");
scanf("%s",&s1.name);
printf("enter the marks \n");
scanf("%d",&s1.marks);
print(s1);
printf("Do you want to store more record");
ans=getch();
while(answer=='y');
}
void print(student s1)
{
printf("\nyou have entered the following student record");
printf("\n %d %s %f",s1.rollno, s1.name, s1.marks);
}
```

Output:

```
Enter the student details
enter the rollno
01
enter the name
Shiva
enter the marks
85
you have entered the following student record
01 Shiva 85.000000
Do you want to store more record
n
```

4.8 Type definition

- Typedef is a statement which allows you to create new data type from an existing data type.
- The new data type has a different name but same characteristics as of the existing data type.
- You can create the new data type from both **predefined data type** such as **int, char, float** and **user defined data type** such as **structure**.
- You can also use the new data type to declare the variables and arrays of original data type.
- The scope of new data type created is limited only within the function in which it is created.
- The syntax of typedef statement is as follows:

typedef old_data_type new_data_type;

where,
typedef is a keyword
old_data_type is the name of the original data type
new_data_type is the name of the new data type

example:

```
typedef int integer;
integer a,b,c;
integer arr[10];
```

```
#include<stdio.h>
#include<conio.h>
#include<stdlib.h>
struct employee
{
int emp_id;
char name[20];
float salary;
```

```
};
typedef struct emp employee;
employee emp1;
clrscr();
printf("Enter the employee ID: \n");
scanf("%d,&emp1.emp_id);
printf("Enter the name of the employee : \n");
scanf("%s,&emp1.emp_id);
printf("Enter the salary of the employee : \n");
scanf("%f,&emp1.salary);
printf("Employee details \n");
printf("Employee ID: %d\n",emp1.emp_id);
printf("Name: %s\n",emp1.name);
printf("Salary: %4.2f\n",emp1.salary);
}
```

Output:

```
Enter the employee ID:
101
Enter the name of the employee :
Shiva
Enter the salary of the employee :
60000
Employee details
Employee ID: 101
Name: Shiva
Salary: 60000.00
```

File Management

- The data stored in the program variables are temporary in nature, exists till the execution of the program. Such data are usually stored in the main memory of a computer and lost when the program is terminated or the power is turned off.
- This can be avoided by storing the data permanently in the

memory, such as hard disk, floppy disks or any secondary storage devices. It is stored as data files, also known as flat files.

- The approach of storing data in files is known as file-oriented approach.
- **File management** or **File handling** refers to the process of writing data to a file, reading data from a file, and performing other operations on files.

4.9 Defining Files:

- In word processors,data is usually stored in documents. Similarly, in programming, files are created to store the data of programs or applications.
- Files are defined for the following purposes:
    - Reading the data.
    - Processing the data.
    - Writing the data.

4.10 Basic Operations on files:

- While working with a document using a word processor, you can perform the following operations.
    - Creating a new document.
    - Writing data in the document.
    - Opening the document.
    - Reading the data from the document.
    - Saving the document.

- In programming, you can perform the following operations on files:
    - Opening a file, if none exists, creating a new file.
    - Reading the data from the file.
    - Writing data to the file.
    - Determining the end of the file.
    - Closing the file.

4.11 Opening and Closing of files:

- The fopen () function is used to open a file.
- When you open a file, you establish a connection between your program and the file being opened.
- The syntax:

  fop=fopen=("filename","mode of opening");

- In the preceding syntax, fop is a pointer of FILE type and refers to a file, and filename is the name of the file to be opened. The mode of opening can be any of the modes as given in table.

Mode of Opening a File	Description
w	Creates a new text file. If the file already exists then its data is deleted.
r	Opens a text file in read-only mode.The file must exist.
a	Opens a text file to append the new data. If the file does not exist then the file is created.
w+	Creates a text file to perform read and write operations. If the file already exists then its data is deleted.
r+	Opens a text file to perform read and write operations. The file must exist.
a+	Opens a text file to perform read and write operations. If the file does not exist then it is created and if it exists then new data is appended at the end of file.

wb	Creates a binary file. If the file already exists then its data is deleted.
rb	Opens a binary file in read-only mode. The file must exist.
ab	Opens a binary file to append the new data. If the file does not exist then the file is created.
wb+	Creates a binary file to perform read and write operations. If the file already exists then its data is deleted.
rb+	Opens a binary file to perform read and write operations. The file must exist.
ab+	Opens a binary file to perform read and append operations. If the file does not exist then the new data is appended at the end of the file.

- The fclose( ) function is used to close a file. Closing a file means removing the connection from the program and saving its content.
- The syntax :

  fclose(fp);

  fop is a pointer of **FILE** type and refers to the file to be closed.

4.12 File Input and Output Operations:

- C offers few functions that can be used to perform input and output (I/O) operations on a file. Such functions are called I/O functions.

i. **fgetc( ) function:**

✓ You can read or write a single character at a time from a file using the fgetc( ) function.
✓ Reading a single character at a time is useful in scenarios where you need to keep track of every single character instead of reading an entire string.
✓ fgetc( ) function takes a file pointer as parameter and returns an int value.
✓ Syntax:

int fgetc(FILE *fp);

✓ While reading if you reach the end of file, then this function returns **"EOF"**.
✓ **EOF** is a constant that indicates that you have reached the end of the file.

ii. **fputc( ) function:**

✓ fputc( ) function is used to write a character at a time to file.
✓ This function is useful if you need to copy a file character by character.
✓ Syntax:

int fputc(int c, FILE *fp);

iii. **fgets( ) function:**

✓ fgets( ) function reads entire line from a file.
✓ Syntax:

fgets(buffer, n, inputfile);

✓ In the preceding syntax, buffer reads to a pointer to a character array and n is the maximum number of characters that can be read from a file.
✓ This function recalls an entire line into buffer till it finds a newline character or till n character.
✓ This function places a NULL character at the end of the buffer.

- ✓ fgets( ) function never stores a newline character into buffer.

iv. fputs( ) function:

- ✓ fputs( ) function write an entire line from a file.
- ✓ fputs( ) function writes characters in buffer till it finds a NULL character.
- ✓ fputs( ) function appends a new line character after a line is added to the output file.
- ✓ Syntax:

fputs(buffer,outputfile);

v. fscanf( ) function:

- ✓ fscanf( ) function works similar to function like scanf( ).
- ✓ fscanf( ) function reads the files.
- ✓ fscanf( ) function works only on files.
- ✓ Syntax:

fscanf(inputfile, "ControlString", &addressvariable);

vi. fprintf( ) function:

- ✓ fprintf( ) function works similar to function like printf( ).
- ✓ fprintf( ) function writes the data to an output file.
- ✓ fprintf( ) function works only on files.
- ✓ Syntax:

fprintf(outputfile, "variable");

- ✓ eg., fprintf(name.txt, "shiva");

Questions:

1. What is structure?
2. Differentiate between an array and structure.
3. How do you access members of a structure?
4. What is need of an array of structures. Explain with example.
5. Write C program to accept name, date of birth, age, salary, height and employment details and display it in attractive manner.
6. How is structure initialized.
7. How can structure member processed?
8. What is file pointer? What is its purpose.
9. Explain the syntax for opening and closing a file.
10. Explain the function to read the string from file.
11. Explain fscanf and fprintf functions. Compare them with scanf and printf function.
12. Write note on error handling.

Module 5:

Pointers and Pre-processors and Data Structures.

5.1 Definition of Pointers

- A Pointer is a variable which holds the address of another variable such as arrays, structures, unions and functions which elsewhere stored in the computer memory.
- A Pointer variable contains only address or memory location of the variable and not the value of a variable.
- Pointers are generally used to point the variables.
- **Advantages of pointers:**

i. Pointers can be used to point different data structures.

ii. Pointers are used with functions to return multiple values.

iii. Pointers are used for dynamic memory allocation.

iv. Pointers are used to achieve the clarity and simplicity.

v. Pointers are used for more compact and efficient coding.

vi. Pointers are used for manipulation of the data at different memory locations easier.

- **Operators used with Pointers:**

i. **The address operator (&):** It gives the address of the variable.

ii. **The indirection operator (*):** It gives the value of that pointer is pointing to.

5.2 Declaration of Pointer

- A pointer variable should also be declared like the normal a variable.
- A pointer is a variable which stores the address of another variable, when it is declared, the compiler allocates the memory only for the pointer but not for type to which it points.
- Both, a pointer variable and variable to which pointer variable points to, must be declared.
- A pointer variable must be assigned the address of the declared variable before used in the program.
- The syntax is:

data_type *pointer_variable_name;

where,

data_type refers the type of pointer variable you declare.

asterisk * symbol notifies the compiler that you are creating a pointer variable.

***pointer_ variable_name** refers the name of the pointer variable.

- Example:

```
int *ptr;

float *temp;
```

Write a program to illustrate the pointer declaration.

```
#include<stdio.h>
#include<conio.h>
main()
{
```

```
int *ptr;
int a=25;
clrscr();
ptr=&a;
printf("\n The value of a is %d",*ptr);
printf("\n The pointer address is %d",ptr);
getch();
}
```

Output:

The value of a is 25

The pointer address is 12

5.3 Address of (&) Operator:

- Memory is the sequential collection of storage cells, each cell has associated address.
- Once the variable is declared, the operating system allocates the memory according to size of data type of that variable.
- eg., int x=120;

For above eg operating system allocates the two bytes of memory and stores 120 in that location since the data type is integer.

- Here, x is variable name, 120 is value of the variable and 1030 is address of the memory location.
- Using the address of (&) operator, you can determine address of a variable.

```
main()
{
int x=120;
```

```
printf("\n Address of x=%d", x);
}
```

5.4 Initializing a Pointer Variable:

- Like the ordinary variable, pointers can be explicitly initialized within the declaration part of the program.
- Pointers are initialized by assigning the address of another variable that are used in the program.
- The syntax:

  data_type *pointer_variable=expression;

  where,

  data_type refers to any basic data type.

  ***ptr** refers to pointer.

  expression can be constant or variable.

Write a program to illustrate the pointer initialization.

```
#include<stdio.h>
void main()
{
int x=123, *ptr;
ptr=&x;
printf("The value of the x=%d",*ptr);
*ptr=300;
printf("\nThe value of the x after pointer initialization=%d", *ptr);
}
```

Output:

The value of x=123

The value of the x after pointer initialization=300

5.5 Pointers and Functions:

- Pointers can be used in function by passing them as parameters to functions.
- Ability to pass pointers to function is very useful and helps to easily represent complex function in C program.
- Pointers can be passed as arguments by two methods,
    i. Call by value.
    ii. Call by reference.

i. **Call by value:**

- Whenever you access a function, a link is established between the actual and formal parameters.
- When the values of the arguments are passed from a calling function to a called function, a temporary storage is created where the actual actual parameters are stored ie., values of actual parameters of calling the function is copied into the corresponding formal arguments of the called function.
- **Program to illustrate the call by value mechanism:**

```
#include<stdio.h>
#include<conio.h>
void swap(int i, int j)
{
int temp;
temp=i;
i=j;
j=temp;
```

```
printf("\n i=%d j=%d", i,j);
}
main( )
{
int x=25,y=30;
clrscr();
swap(x,y);
printf("\n x=%d y=%d", x,y);
getch();
}
```

Output:

```
i=30 j=25
x=25 y=30
```

ii. **Call by reference:**

- In this mechanism, it allows you to copy the address of the actual arguments of the calling function to the formal arguments of the called function.
- In this pointers are passed as arguments to functions.
- In calling program, the function is invoked with the function name and address of actual parameters enclosed within the parenthesis.

  function_name(&var1, &var2, ... &varn);
  where,
  var1, var2,. . . . . varn are actual parameters.
- In the parameter list of the called program each and every formal parameter must be preceded by an indirection operator (*).

  data_type function_name(*var1, *var2, ... ,*varn)
  where,
  data_type is the data type of return value.
  function_name is the name of function.

***var1, *var2, ... ,*varn** are formal parameters

- **Program to illustrate the call by value mechanism:**

```
#include<stdio.h>
#include<conio.h>
void swap(int *i, int *j)
{
int temp;
temp=*i;
*i=*j;
*j=temp;
main( )
{
int x=25,y=30;
clrscr();
swap(&x,&y);
printf("\n x=%d y=%d", x,y);
getch();
}
```

Output:
x=30 y=25

5.6 Pointers and Arrays:

- The array is a set of homogeneous elements, located continuously in memory.
- Pointers can be used with arrays for efficient programming and array name is pointer to the first element in the array.

5.6.1 Pointer and One-dimensional array

- The name of an array itself designates some memory location and that location in main memory is the address of the very first element of the array.

- An array name is pointer to the first element in the array.
- Consider, **int array={1,2,3,4,5};**

Here, we have array containing 5 integers each of these integers is referred by subscript. **ie., array[0] through array[4]**

- We can alternatively access through pointer as follows:

  int *ptr;

  ptr=&array[0];

- **Program to illustrate relationship between array and pointer.**

```
#include<stdio.h>
int array={1,2,3,4,5};

int *ptr;

void main( )
{
int i;
ptr=&array[0];
printf("\n");
for(i=0;i<5;i++)
{
printf("array[%d]=%d", i, array[i]);
printf("\t ptr+%d=%d\n", *(ptr+i));
}
}
```

Output:

```
array[0]=1    ptr+0=1
array[1]=2    ptr+1=2
array[2]=3    ptr+2=3
array[3]=4    ptr+3=4
array[4]=5    ptr+4=5
```

5.7 Operations on Pointers:

5.7.1 Pointer Assignment

- Assignment operation can be done on pointer variables in different ways,

- assigning the address of another variable to pointer variable.

  eg., int *ptr, a;

  ptr=&a;

- You can also assign one pointer variable to another pointer variable when both point to the object of the same data type.

  eg., float *ptr1, *ptr2;

  ptr1=ptr2;

- You can also assign the null value to a pointer variable.

  eg., int *ptr;

  ptr=NULL;

- **Program to illustrate pointer assignment.**

```
#include<stdio.h>

int main(void)

{

int var=50;

int *p1,*p2;
```

```
p1=&var;
p2=p1;
printf("Values at p1 and p2 are: %d %d",*p1,*p2);
printf("Addresses pointed to by p1 and p2 are: %p %p",
p1,p2);
return 0;
}
```

5.7.2 Pointer Comparision

- You can compare the pointer variables by using the relational operators, such as <, >, <=, >=, and !=.
- Pointers variables are compared using the relational expression.

  eg.,

  p1>p2, p1==p2, p1!=p2

- **Program to illustrate pointer comparision.**

```
#include<stdio.h>
#include<conio.h>
main( )
{
int *p1,*p2;
static int arr[6]={1,2,3,4,5,6};
clrscr( );
p1=&arr[2];
```

```
p2=&arr[4];
printf("The address of arr[2] is %d \n",p1);
printf("The value of arr[2] is %d \n",*p1);
p1=p1+3;
printf("The address of p1 is %d \n",p1);
printf("The value of pointed by p1 is %d \n",*p1);
if(p1<p2)
printf("The address %d is less than address %d \n",p1,p2);
else
printf("The address %d is grater than or equals to the address %d \n",p1,p2);
getch();
}
```

Output:

The address of arr[2] is 174

The value of arr[2] is 3

The address of p1 is 180

The value of pointed by p1 is 6

The address 180 is grater than or equals to the address 178

5.7.3 Pointer Conversion

- Pointer of one type can be assigned to pointer of another type by using the pointer conversion.
- There include two types of conversion:

- Using the void * pointer.
- Without using the void *pointer.

- It is allowed to assign the void * pointer to any other pointer. Also, any other pointer can be allowed to assign for void *pointer. This void * pointer is called the **generic pointer**.
- For all other types of pointer conversions, it is performed using the explicit cast.
- eg.,

```
#include<stdio.h>
int main(void)
{
double x=10.5,y;
int *p;
p=(int *)&x;
y=*p;
printf("The value of x is %f",y);
return 0;
}
```

- In the above example, we can see that an explicit cast is used for assigning the address of x to p, which is an int * pointer.

5.7.4 Pointer Arithmetic

- C allows to add integer to pointers.
- Allows to subtract one pointer from another.
- Arithmetic operation on pointer refers to addition and subtraction operations, you can add or subtract the integer values from a pointer variable.
- Both the addition and subtraction have different behaviour according to size of the data type.
- eg.,

```
int i=2, *j,*k;

j=&i;

j=j+1;

j=j+2;

k=j+3;

j=j-2;

k=j-1;
```

- Subtraction of one pointer variable to another pointer variable can be performed only when both variables point to elements of the same array.

- You cannot perform the following operations on pointers:

  - Multiply a pointer with a constant.

  - Add two pointers.

  - Divide a pointer by a constant.

5.8 Pointer to Pointer:

A Pointer is a variable that holds the address of another variable. We can have pointer to point another pointer to target the value. This is called as Pointer to Pointer. In the normal case, pointer holds the address of an object that contains the desired value. In the case of the pointer to pointer, first pointer contains address of second pointer which in turn points to the object containing value.

Declaration used for pointer to pointer,

int **p;

Single asterisk (*) is used to point normal pointer, Double asterisk

(**) is used to point the pointer to pointer.

Example: Program to demonstrate the use of pointer.

```
#include<stdio.h>
int main(void)
{
int n,*p,**q;
n=50;
p=&n;
q=*p;
printf("%d",**q);
return 0;
}
```

OUTPUT:

50

5.9 Dynamic Memory Allocation methods:

- In some languages like BASIC, it is possible to input the size of the array during the execution. This process of allocation of memory size at runtime is referred as **dynamic memory allocation**.

- In C, there are four library routines, memory management functions for the purpose of memory management.

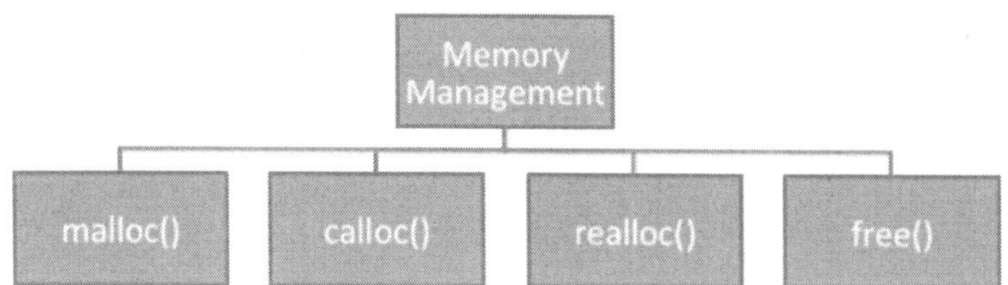

malloc():

- It allocates the block of memory from a pool and returns a void pointer to the first byte of the allocated memory of specified size.
- Free pool refers to a memory that is not used by the program.
- The syntax of malloc() is as follows:

  malloc(size_t size);

  where,

  size_t is defined in the <stdlib.h> header file. It is usually an unsigned integer.

- You can also use the sizeof() operator to specify the number of bytes to be allocated.
- It returns to a block of contiguous memory of specified size.
- The memory allocation can be done as:

  char *p;

  p=malloc(10*sizeof(int));

  Here, after the assignment pointer points to he first 20 bytes of free memory.

  The pointer is actually of char* type, but it can be cast into any other type as per requirement.

calloc():

- calloc() function can be used for both, for the allocation of memory for array elements and to initialize them to 0 and returns the pointer to memory.
- The syntax of the calloc() function is as follows:

ptr= (cast-type *) calloc(n,element_size);

Here, it allocates the memory space for n blocks in bytes where each block is of size specified in element_size.

- calloc() function initializes all bytes to 0 and returns a pointer to first byte of allocated space.

realloc():

- **realloc() function is used to modify the size of previously allocated memory block**
- The syntax of the realloc() function is as follows:

ptr= relloc(ptr,new_size);

Here, it allocates new memory space of the size specified in new_ size to the ptr variable.

- It returns the pointer to the first byte of the new memory block, new size may be smaller or larger than the former size.
- If the function is unsuccessful in locating additional memory block, it returns a NULL value and the original block is lost.

free():

- The free() function is used to free the memory that has been allocated by the malloc() and calloc().
- If the memory allocated is no more required, the memory can be freed using this function.
- The syntax of free() function is as follows:

free(ptr);

where, ptr is pointer created by the malloc() or calloc().

Introduction to Preprocessors

- C compiler has made up of two functional parts: pre-processor and translator.
- The pre-processor is the program that processes the source code before compiling and translating it into a machine language.
- Preprocessor statements provided in the program are not program statements, they are the directives of the processor.
- Preprocessor statements act as a separate program that is invoked by the compiler before translating the program.
- Translator then accepts the source program and converts into machine code to generate an object module.The pre-processor allows to insert, include, exclude and replace text based on the commands provided by the programmer.
- In source code, preprocessors are placed before the main( ) function.
- The three different functions performed by pre-processor are:
    - Used to specify which header files are to be included in the program.
    - Used for the macro definition, enables to create macros to use in the program.
    - Used to conditionally include and exclude code from the program.

The different directives can be categorized under the three types:

- The file inclusion directives.
- The macro substitution directives.

➢ The compiler control directives.

5.10 The file inclusion directives:

- These directives refer to those which insert the contents of other source files
- The pre-processor directive **#include** is used to copy the contents of other files into programs.
- The files are usually header files that contain prototype statements and data declarations for the program.
- #include instructs the compiler to read another source file, which is included between the double quotes or angle brackets.

```
eg., #include"stdio.h"

#include<stdio.h>
```

- At this point pre-processor inserts the entire contents of the file into source code of the program.
- The file is searched only in the standard directories.
- Nesting of included files is allowed, that is included file can include other files. However, file cannot include itself. If an included file is not found, an error is reported and the compilation is terminated.
- Example:

```
#include<stdio.h>

#include<conio.h>

void main()

{

clrscr();
```

```
printf("This program demonstrates the use of file inclusion directive");

getch();

}
```

5.11 The macro substitution directives:

- A macro is the formal syntax that can be used to generate statements for use in the program.
- For the C language macro generates C statements.
- There are two main types of macros: Simple and Parametrized.

Simple macro:

- Format for simple macro is:

  #define identifier token(s).

- The **identifier** is the macro name and a **token** which will be substituted each time the identifier is encountered in the source file.
- If a macro is defined once, it can be used as part of definition of other macros.
- The string which is longer than one line can be continued by placing backslash(\) at end of line.
- Usually defined identifiers are in uppercase. eg., #define MACRO
- Everything that is followed macro name is simply treated as text to be substituted for macro name by pre-processor.
- Preprocessor commands are not terminated by semicolons.
  - eg .,

```
#define ROWS 3

#define COLS 4

#define MSG "enter the number"

void main()

{

int arr[ROWS][COLS];

...

...

printf(MSG);

}
```

- **Parameterized Macro:**

- Parameters can be used in macro which strengthen the capability of the macro.

- Opening parenthesis must be placed immediately at the end of a macro name, to include parameters in macro.

#define name(part1, part2, . . .)replacement tokens

- The identifiers inside the parenthesis are formal parameters and are replaced with actual parameters during expansion.

- Example:

```
#define MUL(X,Y)X*Y

int main(void)

{

X=MUL(P,6);
```

```
Y=MUL(Q,X);
..
..
}
```

- **Nested Macro:**

- Nested macro is supported by C, which rescans a line after macro expansion.
- If an expansion result in a new statement with a macro, the second macro will be properly expanded.
- eg.,

```
#define MUL(a,b)(a)*(b)
#define SQ(a)MUL(a,a)
```

5.12 The compiler control directives:

- The macro can be used to control the selective compilations of portions of the program code.
- This is useful in inserting debugging logic in a program and commenting out code.
- Various Conditional compilation commands supported are:

Command	Description
#if	if expression: When true following code is executed
#endif	End of if expression: terminates included statements.
#else	Specifies the alternative code to be included when the the if expression results false

#elif	else-if: Specifies the alternative code when the previous conditional statement results false.
#ifdef	if defined: include the following statements when a macro name is defined by #define.
#ifndef	if not defined: include the following statements when a macro name is not defined

#if , #endif, #else, and #elif directives:

This pre-processor directive behaves similar to C language if statement. The difference is if directive controls whether certain statements are compiled or not and the if statement controls whether these statements are executed or not.

Syntax:

```
#if condition1
statement_block1;
#elif condition2
statement_block2;
..........
#elif condition_n
statement_blockn;
#else
default_statement_block;
#endif
```

In syntax,

#if directive uses the test expression which it evaluates.

statement_block, code that contain multiple C statements including pre-processor directives.

#elif and #else, are the directives which are optional. But #if and #endif are required.

Example:

For #if and #endif:

```
#include<stdio.h>
#include<file1.h>
if((1>0)&&(defined(USD))
#define currencyrate 60
#endif
#if(defined(UKP))
#define currency_rate 100
#endif
void main()
{
int rs;
clrscr();
rs=10*currencyrate;
printf("%d",rs);
getch();
}
OUTPUT:
600
```

For #else:

```
#include<stdio.h>
#include<file1.h>
if(defined(USD))
#define currencyrate 60
#else
#define currencyrate 100
#endif
void main()
{
int rs;
clrscr();
rs=10*currencyrate;
```

```
printf("%d",rs);
getch();
}
```

OUTPUT:

600

For #elif:

```
#include<stdio.h>
#include<file1.h>
if(defined(USD))
#define currencyrate 60
#elif (defined(UKP))
#define currencyrate 100
#else
#define currencyrate 1
#endif
void main()
{
int rs;
clrscr();
rs=10*currencyrate;
printf("%d",rs);
getch();
}
```

OUTPUT:

600

#ifdef directive:

- It allows to check whether macro is defined or not.
- Once the macro is defined, then compiler translates the lines of code that are followed by #ifdef condition.

example:

```
#include<stdio.h>
#include<file1.h>
#ifdef USD
#define currencyrate 60
#endif
#ifdef UKP
#define currencyrate 100
#endif
void main()
{
int rs;
clrscr();
rs=10*currencyrate;
printf("%d",rs);
getch();
}
```

OUTPUT:
600

#ifndef Directive:

- Similar to the #ifdef directive, #ifndef directive also checks whether macro is defined or not.
- The #ifndef directive verifies the opposite condition as verified by the #ifdef directive.

example:

```
#include<stdio.h>
#include<file1.h>
#ifndef USD
#define currencyrate 60
#endif
#ifndef UKP
#define currencyrate 100
#endif
```

```
void main()
{
int rs;
clrscr();
rs=10*currencyrate;
printf("%d",rs);
getch();
}
```

OUTPUT:
100

Introduction to Data Structures

Data is the base of communication. The data must be categorized and should be stored somewhere very efficiently so that retrieval is very easy. Data Structure is the mathematical model of data or it is the way to organize the data. It is not necessary that data must be homogenous, arrays are used to store homogenous data and structures are used to group the heterogenous data elements.

Formally, **Data structure** can be defined as set of domains D, a set of functions F and set of axioms A. This triple (D,F,A) denotes the data structure d.

There are main operations of data structure, some of them are:

- Creating.
- Traversing.
- Counting the elements.
- Printing.
- Looking up an item for editing or printing.
- Inserting.

- Deleting.
- Concatenating.

5.13 Data Types

Data type is type of data which is specified at the time of declaration of variable.

For eg.,
int a, b;
Here, int is the data type that represents numerical value and a,b are identifers or the variables.

There are two types of data types:

i. Primitive data type.

ii. User defined data type.

i. **Primitive data type:** A programmer can use the pre-defined or built-in data structures in the program to define the variables. It is basic structure which is built into the programming language.

a) **Integer data type:** This data type is used to store the integer value in a variable.

eg., int a;

Here, a is the variable name which can store integer value.

b) **Float data type:** This data type is used to store the real values in a variable.

eg., float a;

Here, a is the variable name which can store real value.

c) **Character data type:** This data type is used to store some text or alphabetical information in a variable.

eg., char alpha;

alpha='S';

character to be stored is always written within single quotes.

d) **Double data type:** This data type is used to store numerical information in a variable. Double data type is mainly meant for real values. It is same as float data type but capacity is larger than float data type.

eg., double val;

5.14 Abstract Data Types

The abstract data type is the triple, D- set of domains, F- set of functions and A-axioms. Only what is to be done is mentioned, but not how is to be done. The ADT operations are carried out using the data structure. Various data structures that can be used for ADT are Arrays, Set, Linked list, Stack, Queues etc.,

There is a specific method for writing ADT,

e) ADT should begin with keyword AbstractDatatype followed by name of the data structure.

f) Inside the curly braces, the ADT must be written.

g) Firstly instances must be written which gives the basic idea of the corresponding data structure.

h) Using the preconditions and postconditions, specific conditions that must satisfy before and after execution must be mentioned.

i) Lastly, listing of all the operations is done.

Example: ADT for Arrays

AbstractDataType Array

{

Instances: An array A of some size, index I and total number of elements in the array n.

Operations:

1. Store (): Stores the desired elements at each successive location.

2. Display (): Displays the elements of the array.

}

5.15 Stacks

Stack is ordered linear structure with insertions and deletions are made at only one end. For eg., stack contains the elements 10, 20, 30, 40, 50. The element 50 is bottommost element and 10 is the topmost element.

10
20
30
40
50

Various operations performed on the stack:

- Creation of Stack.

- Insertion or PUSH element into the stack.

- Deletion or POP element from the stack.

Stack Empty operation:

- Intially when stack is created, it is empty and top is initialized to -1.
- Elements are pushed onto the stack and all the elements can be removed from the stack, then stack becomes empty.
- Thus, when stack reaches to -1, stack is empty.

```
int stackempty()
{
if(top==-1)
return 1;
else
return 0;
}
```

Stack Full operation:

- As the elements in stack are going on inserting, stack gets filled.
- It is necessary to check whether stack is full or not before inserting the elements.

```
int stackfull()
{
if(top>=size-1)
return 1;
else
else
return 0;

}
```

PUSH and POP operations:

- PUSH function inserts the new element on top of the stack.

```
void PUSH(int item)
{
top++;
s[top]=item;
}
```

Before inserting the element, it is checked whether stack is full or not. Only if stack is not full then insertion of new element can be achieved by PUSH operation.

- POP function deletes the element at the top of stack.

```
int POP()
{
int item;
item=s[top];
top--;
return item;
}
```

Before performing popping operation, it invokes the stackempty function to check whether the stack is empty or not.

- If it is empty, function generates the error called underflow!
- If the stack is not empty, pop function is performed and returns the element which is at top of the stack.
- Value at the top of stack is stored in some variable item and decrements value of top.

Example: Program for demonstrating various operations on stack.

```
#include<stdio.h>

#include<conio.h>
```

```
#include<stdlib.h>

#define size 5

struct stack

{

int s[size];

int top;

}st;

    int stackfull()
    {
    if(st.top>=size-1)
    return 1;
    else
    return 0;
    }
    void PUSH(int item)
    {
    st.top++;
    st.s[st.top]=item;
    }
int stackempty()
{
if(st.top==-1)
return 1;
else
return 0;
}


int POP()
    {
    int item;
```

```
    item=st.s[st.top];
    st.top--;
    return item;
    }
void display()

{

int i;

if(stackempty())

printf("\n Stack is empty");

else

{

for(i=st.top;i>=0;i--)

printf("\n %d, st.s[i]);

}

}

void main(void)

{

int item, choice;

char ans;

st.top=-1;

clrscr();

printf("\n Implementation of stack");

do
```

```
{
printf("\n Main Menu");
printf("\n1.Push\n 2.Pop\n 3.Display\n 4.Exit");
scanf("%d",&choice);
switch(choice)
{
case 1: printf("enter the item to be pushed");
        scanf("%d",&item);
        if(stackfull())
        printf("\n Stack is full");
        else
        push(item);
        break;
case 2: if(stackempty())
        printf("Empty stack underflow!");
        else
        {
        item=pop();
        printf("\n The popped element is %d",item);
        }
        break;
```

```
case 3: display();
        break;
case 4: exit(0);
}
printf("\n Do you want to continue");
ans=getche();
}while(ans=='Y' ||ans=='y');
getch();
}
```

Output:

```
        Implementation of stack
Main Menu
1.Push
2.Pop
3.Display
4.exit
Enter your choice 1
Enter the item to be pushed 10
Do you want to continue? Y
Main Menu
1.Push
```

2.Pop

3.Display

4.exit

Enter your choice 1

Enter the item to be pushed 20

Do you want to continue? Y

Main Menu

1.Push

2.Pop

3.Display

4.exit

Enter your choice 3

20

10

Do you want to continue? Y

Main Menu

1.Push

2.Pop

3.Display

4.exit

Enter your choice 2

The popped element is 20

Do you want to continue? Y

Main Menu

1.Push

2.Pop

3.Display

4.exit

Enter your choice 2

The popped element is 10

Do you want to continue? Y

Main Menu

1.Push

2.Pop

3.Display

4.exit

Enter your choice 2

Empty stack underflow!

Do you want to continue? N

5.16 Queues

Queue is the ordered collection of elements. It has two ends, front and rear end. The insertions is made from rear end and and deletions are made from front end. It is the First In First Out Structure (FIFO) data structure.

For eg., suppose queue contains the elements 10, 20, 30, 40, 50. The element 50 is at rear end and 10 at front end.

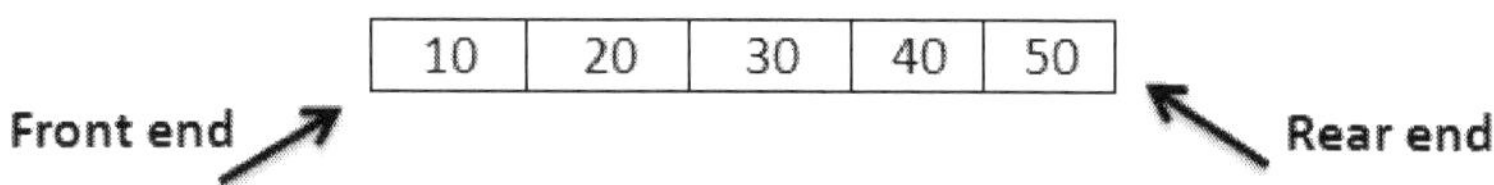

Various operations performed on queue:

- Queue Overflow
- Insertion of element into the queue.
- Queue Underflow.
- Deletion of element from the queue.
- Display of the queue.

Insertion of element into the queue.

The insertion of element into the queue takes place from the rear end.

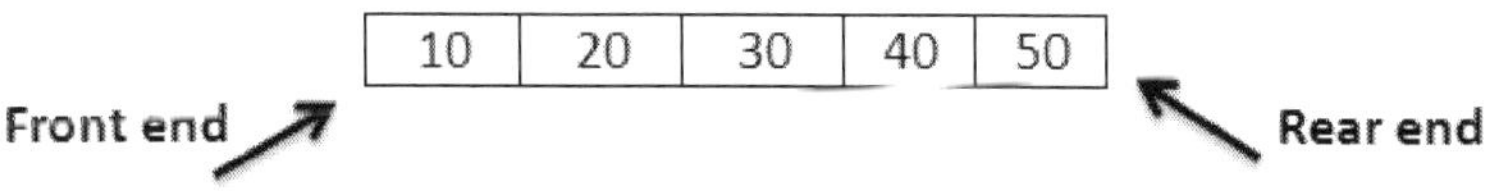

- In the above fig, the element 10 is inserted first next 20, 30, 40 and 50 from the rear end of queue.
- Before inserting the element, should check whether queue is full or not. If the rear pointer exceeds the maximum size of queue, then queue overflow occurs.
- In the above fig, the new element cannot be inserted further as already queue is full and rear is pointing to maximum size.

Deletion of element from the queue:

The deletion of element from the queue takes place by front end.

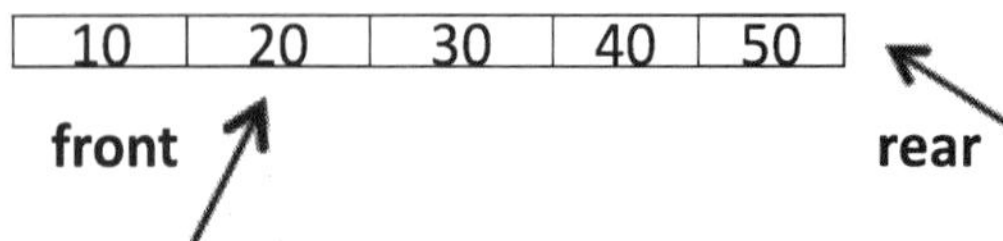

- In the above fig, you can see the element deleted from queue is 10 and then front points to 20.
- Before deleting the element from queue, should check whether queue is empty or not. If the queue is empty, deletion operation cannot be performed. If we attempt o delete the element from the empty queue is called Queue underflow condition.

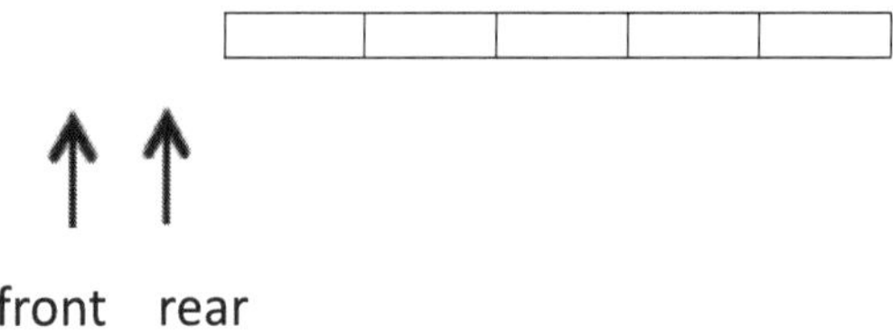

Example: Program for demonstrating various operations on queue.

```
#include<stdio.h>

#include<conio.h>

#include<stdlib.h>

#define size 5

struct queue
```

```
{
int queue[size];
int front,rear;
}Q;
    void qfull()
    {
    if(q.rear>=size-1)
    return 1;
    else
    return 0;
    }
    int insert(int item)
    {
    if(Q.front==-1)
    Q.front++;
    Q.que[++Q.rear]=item;
    return Q.rear;
    }
int qempty()
{
if((Q.front==-1)||(Q.front>Q.rear))
return 1;
else
return 0;
}

int delete()
    {
    int item;
    item=Q.que[Q.front];
    Q.front++;
    printf("\n The deleted item is %d", item);
```

```
    return Q.front;
    }
void display()
{
int i;
for(i=Q.front;i<=Q.rear;i++)
printf("%d",Q.que[i]);
}
void main(void)
{
int choice,item;
char ans;
st.top=-1;
clrscr();
Q.front=-1;
Q.rear=-1;
do
{
printf("\n Main Menu");
printf("\n1.Insert\n 2.Delete\n 3.Display");
printf("\nenter your choice");
scanf("%d",&choice);
```

```
switch(choice)
{
case 1: if(Qfull())
        printf("\n Cannot insert the element");
        else
        {
        printf("enter the number to be inserted");
        scanf("%d",&item);
        insert(item);
}
        break;
case 2: if(Qempty())
        printf("Queue Underflow");
        else
        delete();
        break;
case 2: if(Qempty())
        printf("Queue is empty");
        else
        display();
        break;
```

```
default: printf("\n Wrong Choice");
        break;
}
printf("\n Do you want to continue");
ans=getche();
}while(ans=='Y' ||ans=='y');
getch();
}
```

Output:

```
Main Menu
1.Insert
2.Delete
3.Display
Enter your choice 1
enter the number to be inserted 10
Do you want to continue? Y
Main Menu
1.Insert
2.Delete
3.Display
Enter your choice 1
```

enter the number to be inserted 20

Do you want to continue? Y

Main Menu

1.Insert

2.Delete

3.Display

Enter your choice 3

10 20

Do you want to continue? Y

Main Menu

1.Insert

2.Delete

3.Display

Enter your choice 2

The deleted item is 10

Do you want to continue? Y

Main Menu

1.Insert

2.Delete

3.Display

Enter your choice 3

20

Do you want to continue? N

5.17 Linked List

Linked list is the set of nodes where each node has two fields, data and link.The data field stores information or value and link field points the next node. It is the dynamic data structure.

eg., Fig shows the structure of linked list.

data	link

5.17.1 Representation of Linked list:

```
typedef struct node
{
int data;
struct node *next;
}LL;
```

- The Structure is declared with two members i.e., **data** member and **next** pointer member.
- **data** member can be a character or integer or real depending upon the type of information that a linked list is having.
- **next** member is essentially a pointer type. next holds the address of the next node.

5.17.2 Advantages and disadvantages of linked list:

- Insertion and deletion in linked list can be done efficiently.
- No wastage of memory. Allocation and deallocation of

memory is done as per requirement.

- It does not support random or direct access.
- Each field should be always supported by link field to point next node.

5.17.3 Various operations on linked list:

1. Creation of linked list.
2. Insertion of element into the linked list.
3. Deletion of element from the linked list.

Example: Program for demonstrating various operations on queue.

```
#include<stdio.h>

#include<conio.h>

#include<stdlib.h>

#define MAX 20

int list[MAX];

void main(void)

{

int choice, len,position;

int create();

void display(int);

void reverse(int);

int search(int);
```

```
void delete(int);
do
{
clrscr();
printf("\n Program to perform Operations on linked list");
printf("\n1.Create\n 2.Display\n 3.Search for a number");
printf("\n4.Reverse\n 5.Delete\n 6.Quit");
printf("\nEnter your choice");
scanf("%d",&choice);
switch(choice)
{
case 1: len=create();
            break;
case 2: display(len);
break;
case 3: position=search(len);
break;
case 4: reverse(len);
break;
case 5: delete(len);
break;
```

```
case 6: printf("\n Do you want to exit ?");
ans=getche();
if(ans=='y')
exit(0);
else
break;
default: clrscr();
printf("\n Wrong Choice");
    getch();
}
} while(choice!=6);
}
int  create()
{
int n,i;
clrscr();
printf("\n How many elements you want in list:");
scanf("%d",&n);
if(n>MAX)
printf("\n ERROR: Number of elements exceed the limit");
for(i=0;i<n;i++)
```

```
{
printf("\n Enter the element number %d:",i+1);
scanf("%d",&list[i]);
}
printf("list is created\n");
getch();
return(n);
}
void display(int n)
{
int i;
clrscr();
printf("\n The list is\n");
for(i=0;i<n;i++)
printf("%d\n",list[i]);
printf("\n Press any key to continue\n");
getch();
}
void reverse(int n)
{
int i;
```

```
clrscr();
printf("\n The reversed list is \n");
for(i=n-1;i>=0;i-1)
printf("%d\n",list[i]);
printf("\n Press any key to continue\n");
getch();
}
int search(int n)
{
int i,key;
clrscr();
printf("\n Enter the number you want to search?");
scanf("%d",&key);
for(i=0;i<n;i++)
{
if(list[i]==key)
{
printf("\n The given number is at position %d \n");
getch();
return i;
}
```

```
}
printf("\n The given number is not in the list \n");
getch();
}
void delete(int n)
{
int i;
i=search(n);
list[i]=-1;
printf("\n The element is now deleted");
printf("\n We put -1 to indicate empty location");
getch();
}
```

Output:

Program to perform Operations on linked list

1.Create

2.Display

3.Search for a number

4.Reverse

5.Delete

6.Quit

Enter your choice 1

How many elements you want in list: 5

Enter the element number 1: 10

Enter the element number 2: 20

Enter the element number 3: 30

Enter the element number 4: 40

Enter the element number 5: 50

list is created

1.Create

2.Display

3.Search for a number

4.Reverse

5.Delete

6.Quit

Enter your choice 2

The list is

10

20

30

40

50

Press any key to continue

1.Create

2.Display

3.Search for a number

4.Reverse

5.Delete

6.Quit

Enter your choice 3

Enter the number you want to search? 40

The given number is at position 3

1.Create

2.Display

3.Search for a number

4.Reverse

5.Delete

6.Quit

Enter your choice 4

The reversed list is

50

40

30

20

10

Press any key to continue

1.Create

2.Display

3.Search for a number

4.Reverse

5.Delete

6.Quit

Enter your choice 5

Enter the number you want to search? 30

The given number is at position 2

The element is now deleted

We put -1 to indicate empty location

1.Create

2.Display

3.Search for a number

4.Reverse

5.Delete

6.Quit

Enter your choice 2

The list is

10

20

-1

40

50

1.Create

2.Display

3.Search for a number

4.Reverse

5.Delete

6.Quit

Enter your choice 6

Do you want to exit ? y

5.18 Trees

A tree is a finite set of one or more nodes, such that root node is specially designated node and other remaining n nodes are partitioned into disjoint sets T1, T2,T3,. . . . .Tn are called subtrees of the root.

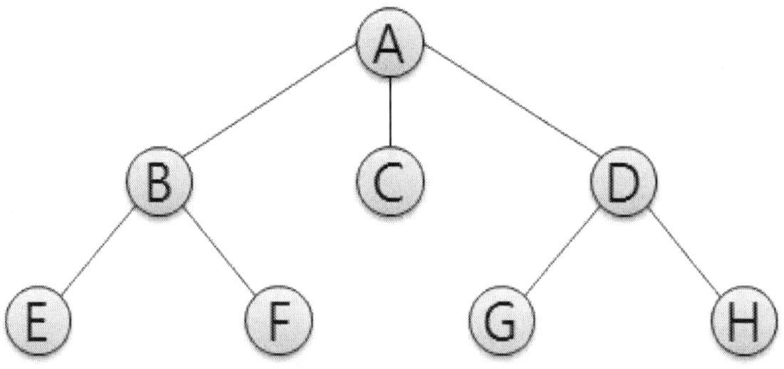

Terms used with tree:

i. **Root:** It is unique node with subtrees attached.

ii. **Parent node:** Node having further sub-branches is called parent node.

iii. **Child node**

iv. **Leaves:** Terminal nodes of the tree.

v. **Sibling:** Node with common parent are called siblings.

vi. **Degree of the node:** Total number of subtrees attached to that node is called the degree of a node.

vii. **Degree of tree:** The maximum degree in the tree is degree of tree.

viii. **Level of the tree:** Root node is always considered at level zero. Adjacent nodes are supposed at level 1 and so on.

ix. **Height of the tree:** The maximum level is the height of tree. It is also called depth of tree.

Questions:

1. What is pointer? Mention the advantages of pointers.
2. How do you declare a pointer variable? Explain with example.
3. Explain pointer initialization with an example.
4. Write the C program to accept array of elements and find the largest element using the pointer.
5. What do you mean by pointer to pointer?
6. What is meant by dynamic memory allocation? List the various library functions used for the dynamic memory allocation.
7. List the compiler control directives.
8. List the commonly used pre-processor directives

Computer Programming Lab

16CPL16/26

Computer Fundamentals Laboratory
Part A
Session I and Session II
Part B
Laboratory Programs

Laboratory Session 1

Computer: An electronic device which takes input from the user, which processes it and gives you the required result in the form of display or print (Output). Computer performs three basic operations

- Taking the input in the form of instruction and data.
- Processing the instruction and data and store the results.
- Display the stored results or output it into the print format.

Hardware: The physical parts of the system, which can be seen and touched by the user.

Software: It is an application program, which performs some operations and gives you desired results.

Network: It is group of interconnected computers or devices to have communication within them.

Programming Language: A software or design logic that controls the system. Use to create application and system software's.

Operating System: A set of software programs supplied along with hardware for the effective and easy use of machine.

Main Parts of Computer System

- Monitor
- CPU
- Keyboard and mouse
- Motherboard
- Hard drive
- Random Access Memory (RAM)
- Processor
- Network card, graphic card, sound card
- DVD-ROM drive
- SMPS etc.

Generations of Computers

Generation of computers came into the mind, when humans were unable to perform some large calculations. So they created a calculating machine called as computers. As the needs of humans gone on increasing, there was development in the computer system.

First Generation (Mid 1940's)

- Computers were using Vacuum tubes (Valves) as an electronic component.
- Machine language was used.
- Input was given through punch cards, paper tapes and results in the form of printouts.
- Computers were as big as room in size.
- Cost was very high.

Second Generation (1956)

- Vacuum tubes were replaced by the transistors.
- Size of transistors was much smaller than vacuum tubes.
- Assembly language was used.
- Consumed less power, faster and reliable.
- Size of computers was reduced.
- Price of computers were also reduced.

Third Generation (1964)

- Integrated Circuits(IC's) made up of small crystal of silicon semiconductor were used.
- Structured programming language C and COBOL was used.
- Speed and efficiency were increased.
- Inputs were given through keyboards and output through monitors.
- Size of computers, power consumption, heat generation and cost were decreased in greater extent.

Fourth Generation (1971 and present)

- Microprocessor chip were used, made up of thousands of Integrated Circuits build on a single silicon chip.
- Object oriented programming language and domain specific language SQL for database access.
- High processing speed, high reliability and low power consumption.
- Size and cost of computers were cut down.

Fifth Generation (Present and future)

- Computers those are dealing with Artificial Intelligence

(AI), expert systems and robotics are in 5th generation.
- These computers are still in development phase.
- Main goal is to respond to the natural language.
- Use of Quantum, Molecular and Nano technology is going to change the face of computers in coming years.

Types of Computers

Types of computers are based upon the purpose, functioning and size of the computer. Accordingly they are classified into four types:

- Super computers
- Mainframe computers
- Mini computers
- Micro computers

Super Computers

- Most powerful computers characterized as fastest, very high processing speed and of large data storage.
- Specifically used for complex applications by big organization.
- Good example is NASA and ISRO uses supercomputers to track and control space discovery.

Mainframe Computers

- Capable of performing high processing speed and data storage but not powerful as super computers.
- Wired in air-conditioned rooms.
- Example: ISP providers use mainframe computers to process information about millions of internet users.

Mini Computers

- Less processing speed than mainframe computers.
- Departments of large company's use this type of computers.
- They can handle large database and accounting efficiently.
- Example: Department of computer monitoring the network traffic of whole company.

Micro computers

- Least powerful type of computers but are the most widely

used and growing in the fastest rate.

- Hardware peripherals can be attached easily.
- Includes Desktop computers, Laptops, tablet pc's, Personal Digital Assistants (PDA) etc.

Characteristics of Computer

Speed: Computer speed depends upon the type of processor and bus line architecture used. Good type of processor and bus line architecture can perform billions of operations in one second. Processor speed depends upon the clock speed and speed of computer is measured in terms of GHz (Giga Hertz).

Accuracy: Computer performs millions of operations but within the given input set of instructions and data, the result obtained should be precise one without any errors.

Reliability: Reliable means that they can do their task properly and consistently. Computer communication and components are very reliable and has very less failure rate.

Storage: Two types of storage are used, first is primary storage and second is secondary storage. Primary storage stores the data temporarily for executing the processes i.e. RAM, while secondary storage used for permanent storage of data i.e. hard disk. Some external devices are also used to store data like portable hard disk, pen drives, memory card etc.

Automation: Once a set of program is fed into the computer, then the computer can take decision automatically without interfering with the user. Example: Pen drive drivers are automatically detected and loaded called as auto play.

Versatility: Computers are capable of performing various operations at same time. Like you are reading this webpage and downloading two files from the internet and also printing the documents simultaneously.

Diligence: Computer can work lot of hours with same speed and accuracy on each operations, without getting tired.

Limitations:

- Computer are not intelligent, they need to be programmed to do their task.
- They cannot learn from their experience.

Block Diagram along with Computer Component!

The basic components of a computer are:

- Input Unit
- Output Unit
- Memory / Storage Unit
- Arithmetic Logic Unit
- Control Unit
- Central Processing Unit

When a computer is asked to do a job, it handles the task in a very special way:

- It accepts the information from the user. This is called input.
- It stored the information until it is ready for use. The computer has memory chips, which are designed to hold information until it is needed.
- It processes the information. The computer has an electronic brain called the Central Processing Unit, which is responsible for processing all data and instructions given to the computer.
- It then returns the processed information to the user. This is called output.

Input Unit: Input Unit accepts the instructions and data from the outside world. Then it converts these instructions and data in computer acceptable form. After that it supplies the converted instructions and data to the computer system for further processing.

Output Unit: The output unit is just reverse of the input unit. it accepts the result produced by computer, which are in coded form and can't be easily understood by us. Then it converts this coded result into human readable form. After that it supplies the converted results to the outside world.

Memory Unit: The Memory Unit is the part of the computer that holds data and instructions for processing. There are two types of computer memory inside the computer:

- Primary Memory
- Secondary Memory

Primary Memory: Primary storage, presently known as main memory, is the only one directly accessible to the CPU. The CPU continuously reads instructions stored there and executes them as required. However, the primary memory can hold information only while the computer system is ON. As soon as the computer system is switched off or rest, the information hold in primary memory disappears. Also it has limited storage capacity because it is very expensive. It is made up of semiconductor devices.

Secondary Memory: Secondary storage, sometimes called auxiliary storage, is all data storage that is not currently in a computer's primary storage or memory. This is computer memory that is not directly accessible to the processor but uses the I/O channels. It is for storing data not in active use and preserves data even without power, meaning it is non-volatile.In a personal computer, secondary storage typically consists of storage on the hard disk and on any removable media, if present, such as a CD or DVD.

Arithmetic Logical Unit: An arithmetic logic unit (ALU) is a digital circuit that performs arithmetic and logical operations. The ALU is a fundamental building block of the central processing unit (CPU) of a computer.
Most ALUs can perform the following operations:
Integer arithmetic operations (addition, subtraction, and sometimes multiplication and division).

Control Unit: The control unit (often called a control system or central controller) directs the various components of a computer.

It reads and interprets (decodes) instructions in the program one by one. The control system decodes each instruction and turns it into a series of control signals that operate the other parts of the computer.

Central Processing Unit: The control unit and ALU of a computer system are jointly known as the CPU. The CPU is the brain of computer system. It takes all calculations and comparisons in a computer systems and it s also responsible for activating and controlling the operations of other units of computer system.

CPU (Central Processing Unit)

- It's a microprocessor chip developed by Intel, AMD or any other company.
- CPU speed depends upon the clock frequency, higher the clock frequency more number of instructions can be executed per second.
- Clock frequency is measured in MHz or GHz.
- CPU word size is the largest number of bits that can be handled by CPU in one clock cycle. It is 8, 16, 32, 64 or 128 bit.
- This word size value determines number of bit processor i.e. 8-bit processor, 16-bit processor, 32 bit processor etc.
- CPU performance also depends upon the RAM, bus speed and cache size as well.
- Called as heart of the computer.

What it does?

- Executes stored instructions called as program.
- Tells rest of the computer system what to do.
- Executes arithmetic calculation and data manipulation.
- Holds data and instruction which are in the current use.
- Responsible for storing and retrieving information on disks and other media.

Bus Lines

- Printed metal traceses on the motherboard or circuit board called as bus lines.
- CPU communicates with other devices on motherboard

like memory, expansion cards, co-processor and keyboards via bus lines.
- Data is in the form of electrical signals either low current zero or high current one.
- Set of parallel buses is like highway for the data, which increases the computer performance.

Types of buses

Data bus:
- Is a path that connects the CPU, memory and other devices on the motherboard.
- Data is transferred form one system component to another using these lines.
- More number of bus lines increases the speed of data transfer because each bus line can transfer one bit at a time.
- The number of bit processor determines the value of data bus i.e. 32-bit processor has 32-bit data bus.

Address bus:
- Is same like data bus.
- Connection is between CPU and RAM and carries memory address instead of data.
- Number of address bus lines determines maximum number of memory address.

Control Bus:
- Control bus Carries Control Signals to various Components.

Motherboard
- A small or large circuit board inside a cabinet containing most of the electronic components.
- Everything connected to the computer is directly or indirectly plugged into motherboard. Components like CPU, BIOS, ROM, RAM, chips, and CMOS setup information.
- Expansion slots for installing different cards like video,

sound, graphics, and NIC.

- Also contains RAM slots, system chipset, controllers and underlying circuit to tie it together.

Motherboard form factors:

- AT (Advanced Technology)
- Baby AT
- ATX (Advanced Technology Extended)
- Mini ATX
- Micro ATX
- Flex ATX
- LPX (Low Profile Extension) and Mini LPX
- NLX (New Low Profile Extended)

Chipset: A chipset is a group of integrated circuits (microchips) that can be used together to serve a single function and are therefore manufactured and sold as a unit. For example, one chipset might combine all the microchips needed to serve as the communications controller between a processor and memory and other devices in a computer

Operating system (OS): An operating system (sometimes abbreviated as "OS") is the program that, after being initially loaded into the computer by a boot program, manages all the other programs in a computer. The other programs are called *applications* or application programs. The application programs make use of the operating system by making requests for services through a defined application program interface (API). In addition, users can interact directly with the operating system through a user interface such as a command language or a graphical user interface (GUI).
All major computer platforms (hardware and software) require and sometimes include an operating system. Linux, Windows, VMS, OS/400, AIX, and z/OS are all examples of operating systems.

Types of Operating System

Batch Operating System: The users of batch operating system do not interact with the computer directly. Each user prepares his job on an off-line device like punch cards and submits it to the computer operator. To speed up processing, jobs with similar needs are batched together and run as a group. Thus, the programmers left their programs with the operator. The operator then sorts programs into batches with similar requirements.

Time-sharing operating systems: Time sharing is a technique which enables many people, located at various terminals, to use a particular computer system at the same time. Time-sharing or multitasking is a logical extension of multiprogramming. Processor's time which is shared among multiple users simultaneously is termed as time-sharing.

Distributed Operating System: Distributed systems use multiple central processors to serve multiple real time application and multiple users. Data processing jobs are distributed among the processors accordingly to which one can perform each job most efficiently.

Network Operating System: Network Operating System runs on a server and and provides server the capability to manage data, users, groups, security, applications, and other networking functions. The primary purpose of the network operating system is to allow shared file and printer access among multiple computers in a network, typically a local area network (LAN), a private network or to other networks. Examples of network operating systems are Microsoft Windows Server 2003, Microsoft Windows Server 2008, UNIX, Linux, Mac OS X, Novell NetWare, and BSD.

Real Time Operating System: Real time system is defines as a data processing system in which the time interval required to process and respond to inputs is so small that it controls the environment. Real time processing is always on line whereas on line system need not be real time. The time taken by the system to respond to an input and display of required updated information is termed as response time. So in this method response time is very less as compared to the online processing.

Networking

Network: It is group of interconnected computers or devices to have communication within them.

Protocol: Is a set of communication rules and formats for sending and receiving data successful over a network.

Client: Computer or any other device connected to a network that requests and uses resources available from the server.
Server: Computer that shares resources with the clients. E.g.: web server, database server, file server etc.

IP (Internet Protocol) Address: Every computer on the internet has unique numeric address, which is 32 bits for IPv4 and alphanumeric address of 128 bits for IPv6.

Firewall: A program that filters all incoming and outgoing traffic from the computer system, limits access to only authorized user and results a pop-up message dialog when detected a threat.

Wi-Fi (Wireless Fidelity): A local area network that uses high-frequency radio waves to transmit and receive data over a short distances.

Line Configuration: Refers to the way the devices are connected by a link. A link is physical or wireless connection between one or more devices.

Types
Point-to-Point

- Dedicated link between two devices.
- Whole capacity of the channel is reserved.
- Uses actual length of wire or cable to connect two ends.
- Microwave or satellite links can be established.
- Examples: Connection between remote control and

operating device such as CD player, television set, home theater etc.

Point-to-Multipoint

- More than two devices share the same link.
- Capacity of channel is shared spatially or temporarily.
- Allows broadcasting packets over the network.
- Each device is able to communicate with each other.
- Examples: A radio station. Video Conference.

Transmission Modes: Transmission modes define the direction of data transmission between two connected devices.

Types

Simplex

- Its a one-way communication, where data flows only in one direction from sender to receiver.
- Eg. Televisions, radios.

Half-Duplex

- Its a two-way communication, data flows in both direction but sender and receiver can't transmit and receive at the same time.
- E.g.: Walkie-talkies, Citizen Band (CB) radios.

Full-Duplex

- Its a two-way communication, where both sender and receiver can trasmit and receive at the same time.
- E.g.: Telephone talk, client and server communication.

Network Topology

- Topology is the way in which computer network is connected.
- Interconnection configuration to provide efficient communication.
- Arrangement of nodes, cables and connecting devices.

Types

Ring Topology

- Each node connected to each other forming a ring like structure.
- Data packets travel from node to node as there is single path.
- Packet travels until it finds the final destination from node to node.
- Physically it is star topology but logically its a ring topology.

Bus Topology:

- All devices such as server, node, printer are connected to common shared cable called as a bus.
- T-connectors are used to connect each device.
- Buses are bidirectional hence all devices are capable to send and receive signals simultaneously.
- But some buses are unidirectional.
- Messages passes to each node, if it matches to its address it takes it, else it transmits to the next node.
- Bus cable is terminated at each end of node by placing terminators to prevent signal reflecting back.

Star Topology

- All nodes are connected to central hub.
- Hub routes the messages from source to destination.
- It acts like repeater for data flow

Mesh Topology

- Dedicated point-to-point link is established between nodes.
- It requires n(n-1)/2 links to connect n nodes.

Tree Topology

- Central hub or root node is connected to other lower end nodes.
- Central hub manages and functions each node.
- Root node act as a server.

- Lower level nodes can be connected to next lower level.
- Point-to-point configuration wiring for each node.

Types of Network

LAN (Local Area Network)

- Group of interconnected computers within a small area. (room, building, campus)
- Two or more pc's can from a LAN to share files, folders, printers, applications and other devices.
- Coaxial or CAT 5 cables are normally used for connections.
- Due to short distances, errors and noise are minimum.
- Data transfer rate is 10 to 100 mbps.
- Distinguished on their transmission media and topology.
- Example: A computer lab in a school

MAN (Metropolitan Area Network)

- Design to extend over a large area.
- Connecting number of LAN's to form larger network, so that resources can be shared.
- Networks can be up to 5 to 50 km.
- Owned by organization or individual.
- Data transfer rate is low compare to LAN.
- Example: Organization with different branches located in the city.

WAN (Wide Area Network)

- Are country and worldwide network.
- Contains multiple LAN's and MAN's.
- Distinguished in terms of geographical range.
- Uses satellites and microwave relays.
- Data transfer rate depends upon the ISP provider and varies over the location.
- Best example is the internet.

NIC: A Network Interface Card (NIC) is circuit board or a card that allows computers to communicate over a network via cables or wirelessly.

- It is also called as LAN adaptor, network adaptor or network card.
- Enable clients, servers, printers and other devices to transmit and receive data over the network.
- Operates on physical and data link layer of OSI model.
- Every network adaptor is assigned a unique 48-bit Media Access Control (MAC) address, which is stored in ROM to identify themselves in a network or a LAN.
- Available maximum data transfer rate is 10, 100 and 1000 MBPS.
- Typically network adaptor has RJ45 or BNC or both sockets for connecting and a LED to show up it is active and transmitting the data.
- Connects to a network via cables like CAT5, Co-axial, fiber-optics etc. And wirelessly by a small antenna.

Session II

RAM (Random Access Memory):

Definition

- A small scale size IC's memory chip used to store and access data in any order (i.e. in random order), so the name Random Access Memory.

Description

- Also called as temporary or volatile memory.
- Holds the program and data, which are currently processing.
- Data is lost as soon as computer is turned off or power failure.
- Data stored in this memory can be altered or changed.

Types of RAM

SRAM (Static RAM):

- Fast and has less access time.
- Consists of flip-flop using either transistor or MOS

(Mosfet).

- For each bit it requires one flip-flop.
- Status of each bit remains as it is unless there is write operation or power is off. e.g. Cache memory.

Advantages

Refreshing circuit is not required.

Disadvantages

Costly and low package density.

Requires more space.

DRAM (Dynamic RAM):

- Slower and higher access time
- Data is stored in the form of capacitors.
- Capacitors charges when data is 1 and doesn't charge if data is 0.
- Because of leakage current in capacitor, they need to be refreshed to hold the data in memory cells.
- Refreshing is the process in which the contents of each memory cell is read and written hundred times a second.
- This maintains the data of memory cells in capacitor. e.g. Main memory.

Advantages

Cheaper than static RAM.

Disadvantages

Requires refreshing circuit.

SDRAM(Synchronous dynamic random access memory):

SDRAM is (DRAM) that is synchronized with the. Classic DRAM has an asynchronous interface, which means that it responds as quickly as possible to changes in control inputs. SDRAM has a synchronous interface, meaning that it waits for a before responding to control inputs and is therefore synchronized with the computer's system bus. The clock is used to drive an internal that pipelines incoming commands. The data storage area is divided into several *banks*, allowing the chip to work on several memory access commands at a time, interleaved among the separate banks.

This allows higher data access rates than an asynchronous DRAM.

Generations of SDRAM:

SDR SDRAM (Single Data Rate synchronous DRAM)
This type of SDRAM is slower than the DDR variants, because only one word of data is transmitted per clock cycle (single data rate). But this type is also faster than its predecessors and which took typically 2 or 3 clocks to transfer one word of data.

DDR1 SDRAM
DDR SDRAM (sometimes called *DDR1* for greater clarity) doubles the minimum read or write unit; every access refers to at least two consecutive words.

DDR2 SDRAM
DDR2 SDRAM is very similar to DDR SDRAM, but doubles the minimum read or write unit again, to 4 consecutive words. The bus protocol was also simplified to allow higher performance operation. (In particular, the "burst terminate" command is deleted.) This allows the bus rate of the SDRAM to be doubled without increasing the clock rate of internal RAM operations; instead, internal operations are performed in units 4 times as wide as SDRAM.

DDR3 SDRAM
DDR3 continues the trend, doubling the minimum read or write unit to 8 consecutive words. This allows another doubling of bandwidth and external bus rate without having to change the clock rate of internal operations,

DDR4 SDRAM
DDR4 SDRAM is the successor to DDR3 .

Flash memory
Flash memory is a type of constantly-powered nonvolatile memory that can be erased and reprogrammed in units of memory called blocks.
Flash memory is often used to hold control code such as the basic

input/output system (in a personal computer. When BIOS needs to be changed (rewritten), the flash memory can be written to in block (rather than byte) sizes, making it easy to update. On the other hand, flash memory is not useful as random access memory (because RAM needs to be addressable at the byte (not the block) level.

Flash memory is used in digital cellular phones, digital cameras, LAN switches, s for notebook computers, digital set-up boxes, embedded controllers, and other devices.

Hard Disk

Definition

A non-volatile storage device used to store digital data on magnetic surface of rigid plate by using read/write heads.

- It is secondary storage device.
- Standard size is 3.5 inch for desktops and 2.5 inch for laptops
- Modern hard disk uses serial interface like Serial ATA (SATA), Serial Attached SATA (SAS) etc.
- Data rate: it is number of bytes transferred per second to the cpu, varies from 5 - 40 MBPS.
- Seek time: it is amount of time when cpu request a file and time when cpu gets the first byte of the file, varies from 10 - 20 milliseconds.
- Cost of drive is less compare to volatile storage devices like RAM.

Types

Internal Hard Disk

- It is located inside the system case (cabinet).
- Used to store programs and large data files.
- Consists of one or more metallic plates sealed inside a container.
- Container includes a motor for rotating disk.
- It also contains access arm and read/write heads for reading/writing the data.
- Hard disk spins between 3600 to 12,000 rpm.
- Hard disk comes with different storage capacities.

- Its capacities is measured in bytes with common capacities stated as GB or TB.
- Can perform faster operations and has fixed amount of storage.

Internal Cartridges

- To solve problems of internal hard disk, hard disk cartridges came into existence.
- Problem such as they can't be removed from the system cabinet easily.
- These are easy to remove as like CD from CD drive.
- Amount of storage is limited to number of cartridges.
- Used as alternative to internal hard disk.
- Useful to protect or secure information and also to backup of the pc.
- Ranges from 2 GB to 160 GB

Hard Disk Packs

- This type of hard disk are used by big organization to store massive amount of data.
- Their capacity ranges from Peta Bytes (1 PB = 1024 TB).
- Banks and government sectors uses to record finicial information.
- Consists of several platter aligned one above the other.
- They resemble stack of phonograph records.
- There is space between the disks to allow access arm to move in and out.
- Each access arm has two read/write heads.
- One reads the disk surface and other reads surface below it.
- Only one read/write head is activated at given moment.
- Example: Disk pack with 20 disks providing 37 recording surfaces.
- Because the top and bottom outside surfaces of the pack are not used.

Optical Media

- Is a disk drive which uses optical-disc technology to read and write discs.

- Connected to motherboard via IDE (ATA), SCSI, S-ATA, Firewire, or USB interface.
- Burning speed rate is 1x ,4x, 8x, 12x, 24x, 48x, 52x.

CD-ROM

- Stands for Compact Disc Read Only Memory.
- Users can read data from the CD but cannot burn/write their information on CD.

CD Writer

- Users can read and write data to and from the CD.

DVD-ROM

- Users can only read data from the CD and DVD.

DVD Writer

- Users can read and write data from both CD and DVD.

Working

- Consists of three motors.
- First to inject and eject the tray, second for spinning the CD and third to move the laser beam back and forth.
- Uses Optical-disk technology where a laser beam alters the surface of a plastic or metallic disk to represent data.
- Unlike to hard disk, which uses magnetic charges to represent 0 and 1, optical disks uses reflected light.
- On disc surface (CD or DVD) 1's and 0's are represented by flat areas called lands and bumpy areas called pits.
- To read a disc, a laser of tiny beam of light is emitted on the surface area.
- This surface area reflects the light, and amount of reflected light determines whether the area represents a 0 or a 1.
- To write on the disc a tiny laser of beam of light is emitted to heat the layer made-up of organic dye or metallic alloys to form pits. And these alternating lands and pits form the data.
- For CD-R it is heated upto approximate 200°C and for CD-RW approximate 700°C.
- As read and write operation does not touches the surface

of the disc, there is no friction and no wear or risk of disc crashing.

Flash drive

A **flash drive** is a drive using Flash Memory.

Specific flash drive types

- Flash memory-based Compact Flash (CF) card (including CFast card) and XQD Card (Note: some other types of CF and XQD card are not flash memory-based)
- Memory Stick (MS)
- Multimedia Card(MMC)
- Secure Digital card (SD, SDHC, SDXC)
- Smart Media card (SM)
- Solid State Drive SSD, using flash memory (a few SSDs use DRAM or MRAM)
- USB Flash Drive(UFD)
- xD-Picture Card(xD)

Keyboard

Description

- Commonly used input device to enter text.
- Contains various types of keys such as alphanumeric, punctuation and special keys.
- Alphanumeric keys - letters and numbers.
- Punctuation keys - comma, semicolon, point so on.
- Special keys - function keys, control keys, navigation keys so on..
- Control keys that can performs an action(function), when held in combination with another key such as ctrl + a.
- Various layouts are ABCDE, XPeRT, QWERTY and AZERTY but QWERTY and AZERTY are commonly used.
- Wide range of keyboard designs are available such as traditional, ergonomic, folding etc.
- Connecting ways of keyboard are serial port, usb port and wirelessly.
- Every character typed from keyboard is sensed as keystroke by the CPU.

- These keystrokes deposits a scan code which are stored in keyboard interface chip to have synchronization between keyboard and CPU.
- CPU processes these keystrokes and results the output in the form of display or command.

Special shortcuts

- Shift + Delete = Deletes the selected file or folder permanantly without placing in the recycle bin.
- Ctrl + Shift while dragging an item = Creates shortcut of selected item
- Alt + Enter = Shows properties of selected item.
- Alt + Spacebar = Opens the shortcut menu for the active window.
- Alt + Tab = Switches between the open applications.
- Ctrl + Esc = Opens Start menu.
- Holding shift while inserting CD = Prevents the CD from automatically playing.
- Windows logo button + Break = Displays System properties dialog box.
- Windows logo button + D = Shows the desktop.
- windows logo button + M = Minimizes all windows.
- windows logo button + E = Opens My computer.
- Windows logo button + F = Searches for file and folder.
- Windows logo button + L = Logoff the current user.
- Windows logo button + R = Opens run dialog box.
- Windows logo button + F1 = Opens Windows help.
- Ctrl + Windows logo button + F = Searches for computer in the network.
- F2 = To Rename selected item.
- F3 = Search for file or folder.

Mouse

- Controls a pointer that is displayed on the monitor.
- Has usually arrow like shape.
- Can have one or more buttons and a wheel button to scroll over the pages.
- Used to select commands and to control information.

Working of optical mouse:

- Contains a small camera which takes more than thousands of snapshots every second.
- Small LED (light emitting diode) provides light underneath the mouse.
- Helps to highlight slight differences in the surface underneath the mouse.
- These differences are reflected back into the camera for digital processing.
- This comparison finds speed and direction of mouse movement.

Types

- **Mechanical mouse:**
  - It contains a rotating ball on the bottom and attached with a cord to system unit.
  - As it moves the roller rotates and controls the pointer on the monitor.
- **Optical mouse:**
  - Refer working of mouse explained above.
- **Wireless mouse:**
  - Allows cordless access to the computer.
  - Contains a receiver station that uses a PS/2 or USB connection to plug.
  - Transmits data via infrared or radio frequency.
  - Uses alkaline batter as a power supply.

Printers and Plotters

Plotters were the first type of printer that could print with color and render graphics and full-size engineering drawings. As a rule, plotters are much more expensive than printers. They are most frequently used for CAE (computer-aided engineering) applications, such as CAD (computer-aided design) and CAM (computer-aided manufacturing). Hewlett-Packard is the leading vendor of plotters worldwide.

A plotter is a printer that interprets commands from a computer to make line drawings on paper with one or more automated pens. Unlike a regular printer the plotter can draw continuous point-to-point lines directly from Vector Graphics files or commands. There are a number of different types of plotters: a *drum plotter* draws on paper wrapped around a drum which turns to produce one direction of the plot, while the pens move to provide the other direction; a *flatbed plotter* draws on paper placed on a flat surface; and an *electrostatic plotter* draws on negatively charged paper with positively charged toner.

Printers:

- Device that prints text and graphics in the same format and shape which is displayed on the screen connected via printer cable or USB cable.
- Transforms digitally stored documents, graphics, text data on paper/hard copy.
- Speed of printer is measured in printed pages per minute.
- Printers can be shared in the LAN, Wireless networks or Ethernets.
- New types of printers are combined with printing, scanning and fax in a single unit.

Types of Modern Printers

Inkjet Printers:

Sprays small droplets of ink at high speed on the surface. They are reliable, quick, and inexpensive.

1) Continuous Flow:

- Produces continues flow of stream droplets by spraying ink out of the nozzle.
- Stream of ink is broken down into droplets of ink using ultrasonic waves.
- When ink is desired on the medium, only selected droplets are electro statically charged.
- Deflection plates are used to direct the ink onto the medium.
- Remaining ink which is not required is sent back to reservoir through gutter.

2) Drop on demand:

- Ink is sprayed from the nozzle when it is required.

- Ink is fired on medium pressure with the help of piezoelectric crystal.
- When sufficiently high voltage is applied the piezoelectric crystal expands.
- This minimizes the volume of the ink chamber and vice versa for low voltage.
- Color printers consists of three nozzles each for one basic color.

Laser Printers:

Uses laser beam to produce images with excellent text and graphics.

Used in high quality outputs.

Working:

- Consists of drum which is coated with a photo conductive material.
- As drum rotates the coating on drum gets electrically charged.
- Drum remains charged until it is struck by laser light.
- When laser light falls on drum it selectively discharges some area of the drum.
- This forms a negative image on the drum.
- Position of laser light is maintained by rotating polygonal mirror.
- Toner is a black plastic base ink powder.
- This powder gets attracted to the charged areas on the drum.
- Image on the drum is transferred to oppositely precharged paper.
- Toner is fused to the paper by hearing and applying pressure to form a permanent image.

ALGORITHMS AND FLOWCHARTS

Algorithms

- The fundamental knowledge necessary to solve problems using a computer is the notion of an algorithm.
- An algorithm is a precise specification of a sequence of instructions to be carried out in order to solve a given

problem. Each instruction tells us what task is to be performed.

Ex: Algorithm to Find Largest of Three Numbers

Step1: Read three numbers A, B, C

Step2: Compare A with B

Step3: If A is larger compare it with C

Step4: If A is larger than C then A is the largest otherwise C is the largest.

Step5: If A is smaller than or equal to B in the first step then B is compared with C.

Step6: If B is larger than C then B is the largest number otherwise C is the largest number.

Step7: Stop

Flowcharts

A flowchart is a formalized graphic representation of a logic sequence, work or manufacturing process, organization chart, or similar formalized structure. The purposc of a flow chart is to providc people with a common language or reference point when dealing with a project or process.

Pseudo code

An outline of a program, written in a form that can easily be converted into real programming statements.

For example, the pseudo code for a bubble sort routine might be written:

while not at end of list,
compare adjacent elements,
if second is greater than first,
switch them ,
get next two elements,

if elements were switched,
repeat for entire list

Pseudo code cannot be complied nor executed, and there are no real formatting or syntax rules. It is simply one step - an important one - in producing the final code. The benefit of pseudo code is that it enables the programmer to concentrate on the algorithm without worrying about all the syntactic details of a particular programming language. In fact, you can write pseudo code without even knowing what programming language you will use for the final implementation.

Example

```
BEGIN
 INPUT name
 IF name == "Harry" THEN
  OUTPUT "Why don't you marry Pippa?"
 ELSE
  OUTPUT "Are you Royal enough?"
 END IF
END
```

1. Design and develop a flowchart or an algorithm that takes three coefficients (a, b, and c) of a Quadratic equation (ax2+bx+c=0) as input and compute all possible roots. Implement a C program for the possible roots for a given set of coeffiecents with appropriate messages

Algorithm:

Step 1: Start
Step 2: Read ß a , b , c //Read Co-efficient
Step 3: if a=0, b=0, c=0
    Write àInvalid Input
Step 4: dßb*b-4a*c //calculate disc
Step 5: if d=0 //Roots are equal
    Writeà Roots are equal
    root1 ß -b/(2*a) ;
    root2 ß-b/(2*a);
    writeà root1 , root2
    [Goto Step 8]
Step 6: if d>0 // Roots are Real
    Writeà Roots are Real and Distinct
    root1 ß-b +sqrt (d)/ (2*a);
    root2 ß-b +sqrt (d)/ (2*a);
    writeà root1 , root2
    [Goto Step 8]
Step 7: if d<0 // Roots are imaginary
    WriteàRoots are imaginary
    Realß -b/(2*a);
    ImaginaryßSqrt (fabs (d))/(2*a);
    writeà root1 , root2
Step 8: Stop

/* Flow Chart to find different roots of Quadratic Equation*/

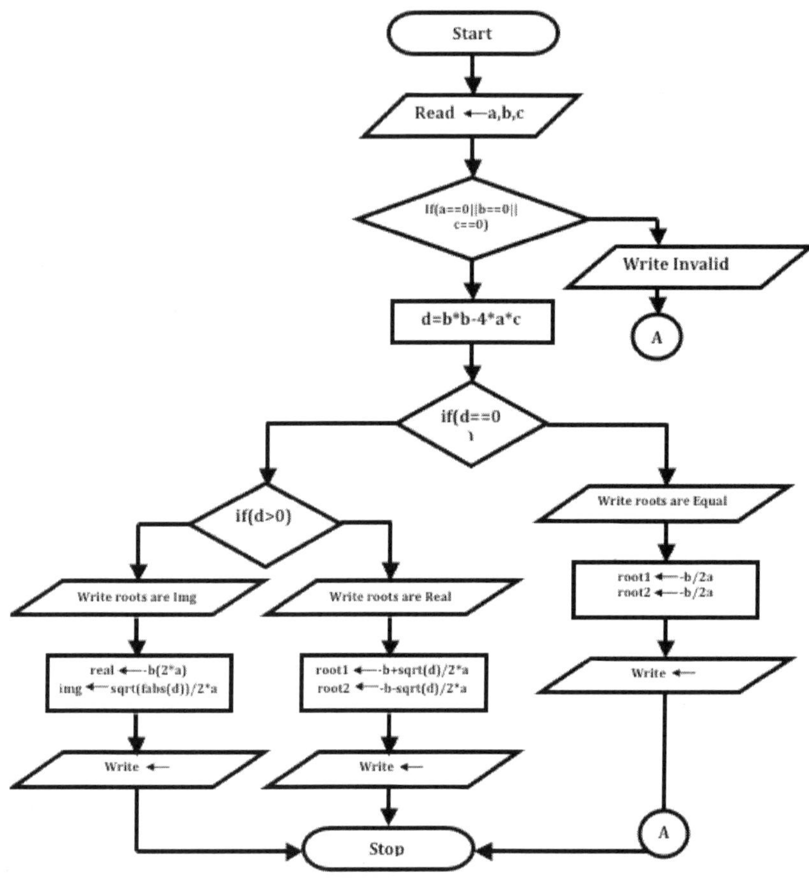

/* Program to find different roots of Quadratic Equation*/

```
#include<stdio.h>
#include<conio.h>
#include<math.h>
#include<stdlib.h>
void main( )
{
        float a,b,c,d,real,imaginary,root1,root2;
        clrscr();
         printf("enter the valve of a,b,c");
```

```
        scanf("%f%f%f",&a,&b,&c);
        if(a==0||b==0||c==0)
        {
                printf("invalid input\n");
                getch( );
                exit(0);
        }
        d=b*b-4*a*c;
        if(d==0)
        {
                printf("roots are equal roots\n");
                root1=-b/(2*a);
                root2=-b/(2*a);
                printf("root1=%f\n",root1);
                printf("root2=%f\n",root2);
        }
        else if(d>0)
        {
                printf("roots are real and distinct\n");
                root1=(-b+sqrt(d))/(2*a);
                root2=(-b-sqrt(d))/(2*a);
                printf("root1=%f\n",root1);
                printf("root2=%f\n",root2);
        }
        else if(d<0)
        {
                printf("roots are imaginary\n");
                real=-b/(2*a);
                imaginary=sqrt(fabs(d))/(2*a);
                printf("root1=%f+i%f\n",real,imaginary);
                printf("root2=%f-i%f",real,imaginary);
        }
        getch( );
}
```

Output

```
Turbo C++ IDE
enter the valve of a,b,c
1
2
0
invalid input
_
```

```
Turbo C++ IDE
enter the valve of a,b,c
1
2
1
roots are equal roots
root1=-1.000000
root2=-1.000000
```

```
Turbo C++ IDE
enter the valve of a,b,c
1
4
1
roots are real and distinct
root1=-0.267949
root2=-3.732051
```

```
Turbo C++ IDE
enter the valve of a,b,c
1
4
9
roots are imaginary
root1=-2.000000+i2.236068
root2=-2.000000-i2.236068_
```

2. Design and develop an algorithm to find the *reverse* of an integer number NUM and check whether it is PALINDROME or NOT. Implement a C program for the developed algorithm that takes an integer number as input and output the reverse of the same with suitable messages. Ex: Num: 2014, Reverse: 4102, Not a Palindrome

Algorithm:

Step 1: Start

Step 2: Read ← num //Read Number

Step 3: temp←num

rev←0 //calculate reverse of a Num

Step 4: while (num>0)

digit←num %10

rev←rev*10+digit

num←num/10

Step 5: write→rev //Print reverse number

Step 6: if(temp==rev) //Check no. is palindrome or not

write→Number is palindrome

else

write→Number is not a Palindrome

Step 7: Stop

/* Flow Chart to find the given number is palindrome or not*/

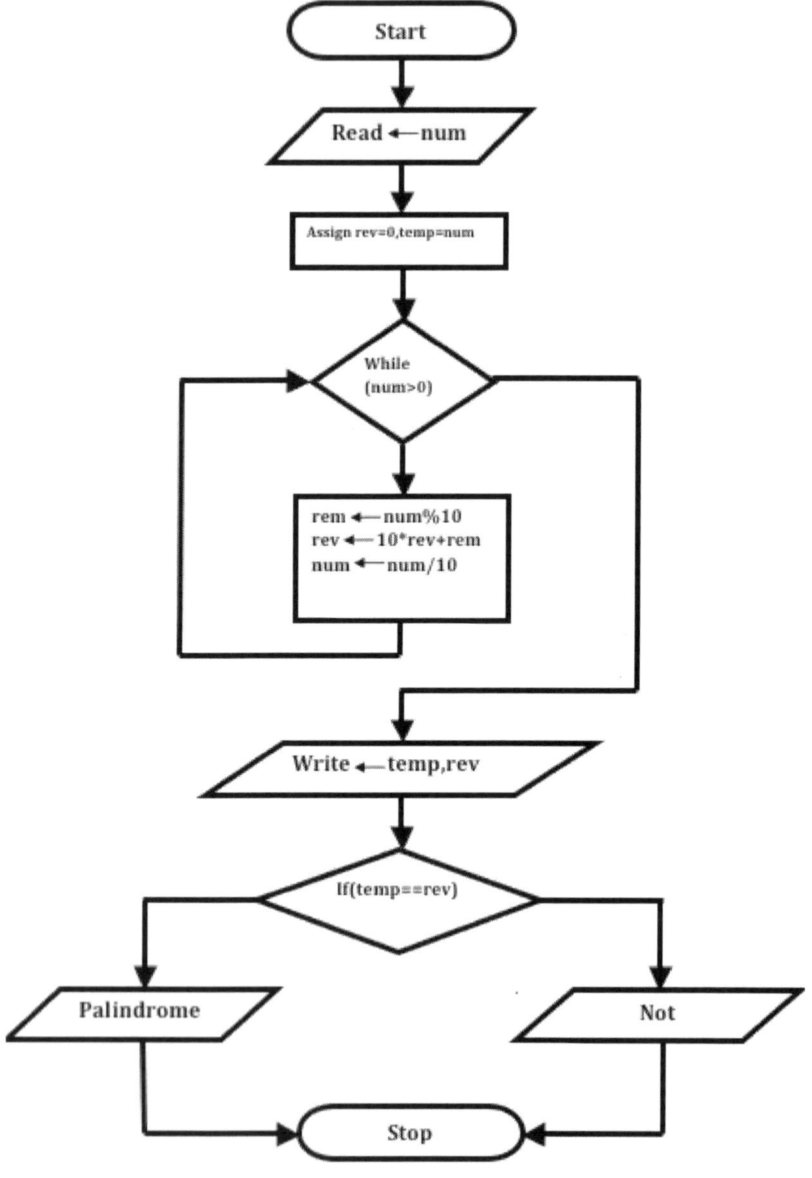

/* Program to find the given number is palindrome or not*/

```
#include<stdio.h>
#include<conio.h>
void main( )
{
        int  num,digit,temp,rev;
        clrscr( );
        printf("enter any integer number");
        scanf("%d",&num);
        rev=0;
        temp=num;
        while(num>0)
        {
                digit=num%10;
                rev=rev*10+digit;
                num=num/10;
        }
        printf("The given number is %d\n",temp);
        printf("reverse of the given number is %d\n",rev);
        if(temp==rev)
        printf("The given number is palindrome");
        else
        printf("The given number is not a palindrome");
        getch( );
}
```

Output

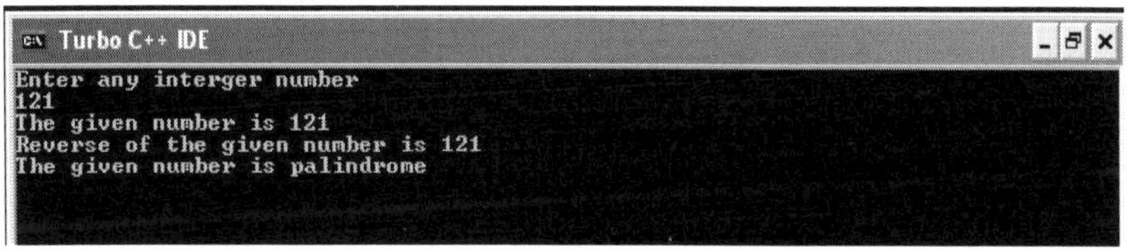

```
Turbo C++ IDE
Enter any interger number
121
The given number is 121
Reverse of the given number is 121
The given number is palindrome
```

Turbo C++ IDE
Enter any interger number
123
The given number is 123
Reverse of the given number is 321
The given number is not a palindrome

3 a. Design and develop a flowchart to find the square root of a given number *N*. Implement a C program for the same and execute for all possible inputs with appropriate messages.

Note: Don't use library function *sqrt(n)*.Algorithm: To find Square root of a given number.

Algorithm:

Step 1: Start

Step 2: Read ← num //Read Number

Step 3: sqroot←num

temp←0

Step 4: while (sqroot != temp) //Calculate square root of Number

temp←sqroot

sqroot ←((num/sqroot) + sqroot)/2

Step 5:write →sqroot //prints square of a number

Step 6: Stop

/*Flow chart to find square root of the given number*/

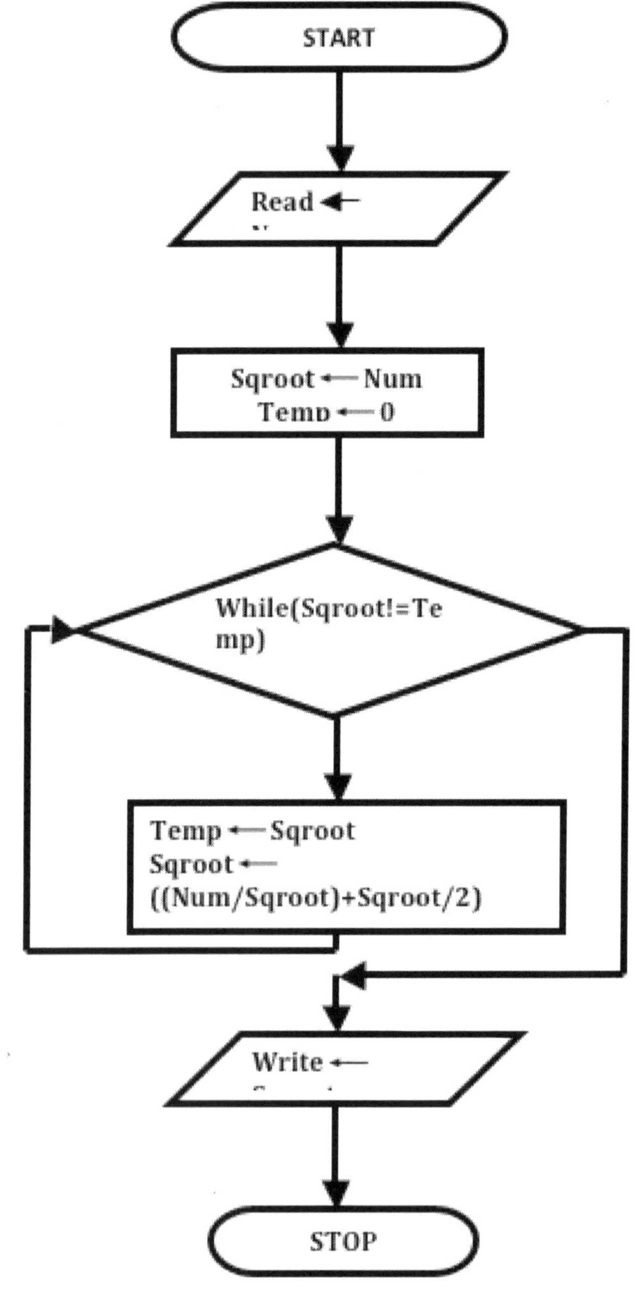

/*Program to find suare root of the given number*/

```
#include<stdio.h>
#include<conio.h>
void main( )
{
        float num, sqroot,temp;
        clrscr( );
        printf("\n enter the number\n");
        scanf("%f",&num);
        sqroot=num;
        temp=0;
        while(sqroot!=temp)
        {
                temp=sqroot;
                sqroot=((num/sqroot)+sqroot)/2;
        }
        printf("%f",sqroot);
        getch( );
}
```

Output

3b. Design and develop a C program to read a *year* as an input and find whether it is *leap year* or not. Also consider end of the centuries.

Algorithm:

Step 1: Start

Step 2: Read ←year //Read year

Step 3:if (year% 4)==0) //Check leap year and centuries

    if((year%100)==0) or ((year%400)==0)
    write →century leap year
    else
    write →normal leap year
    else
    write →given year is not leap year

Step 4: Stop

/*Program to find Leap year or not*/

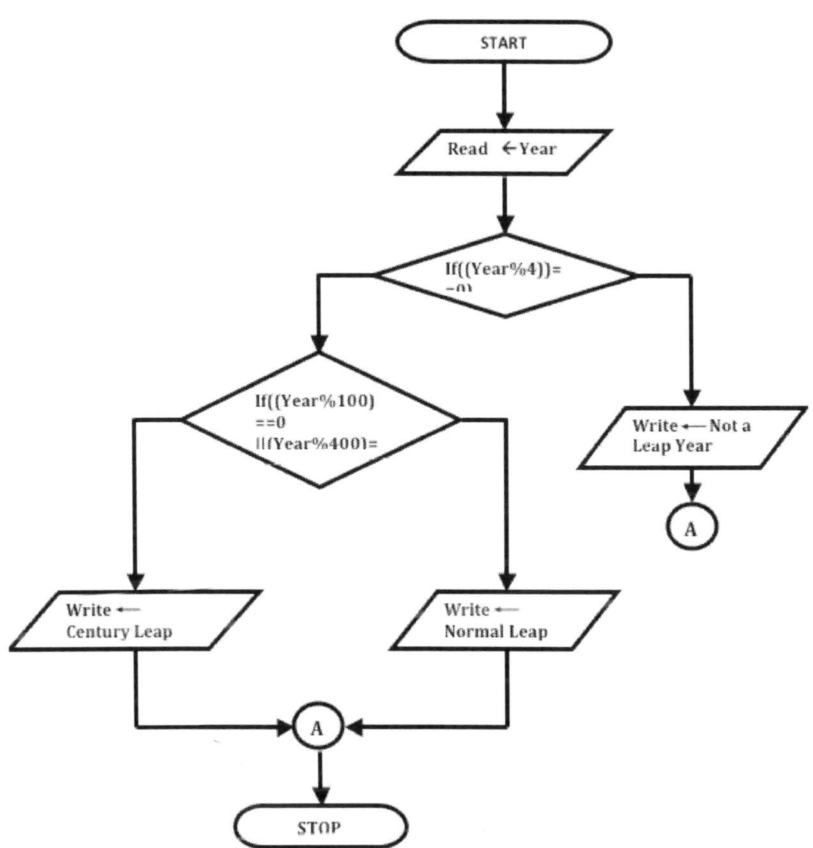

/*Program to find the leap year or not */

```
#include<stdio.h>
#include<conio.h>
void main( )
{
	 int year;
	clrscr( );
	printf("\n enter the year \n");
	scanf("%d",&year);
	if((year%4)==0) //test for leap
	{
		if(((year%100)==0) || ((year%400)==0)) // teat for
Four Centurian Leap
		{
			printf("%d is Centurian Leap year",year);
		}
		else
		{
			printf("%d is leap year but not Centurian
Leap Year",year);
		}
	}
	 else
	{
		printf("\n %d is neither Leap nor Centurian Leap
year\n",year);
	}
	getch( );
}
```

Output

```
Turbo C++ IDE
enter the year
2000
2000 is Centurian Leap year
```

```
Turbo C++ IDE
enter the year
1996
1996 is leap year but not Centurian Leap Year_
```

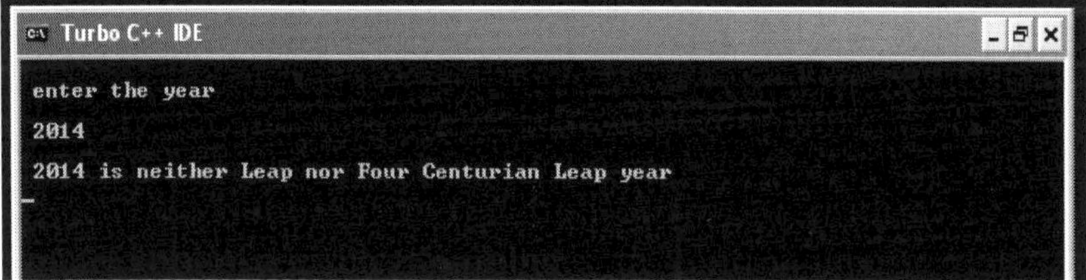

4. Design and develop an algorithm to evaluate polynomial f(x) = $a_4x^4 + a_3x^3 + a_2x^2 + a_1x + a_0$, for a given value of *x* and its coefficients using Horner's method. Implement a C program for the same and execute the program with different set of values of coefficients and *x*.

Algorithm:

Step 1: Start

Step 2: [Read Inputs]

for i =0 to 4

read ← a [i].

end for

read ← x.

Step 3: [initialize]

p = a [4]

Step 4: [evaluate polynomial]

for i = 3 to 0

p = p * x + a [i].

end for

Step 5: [Display results]

p → Write.

Step 6: Stop.

/*Flow Chart to find the Polynominal */

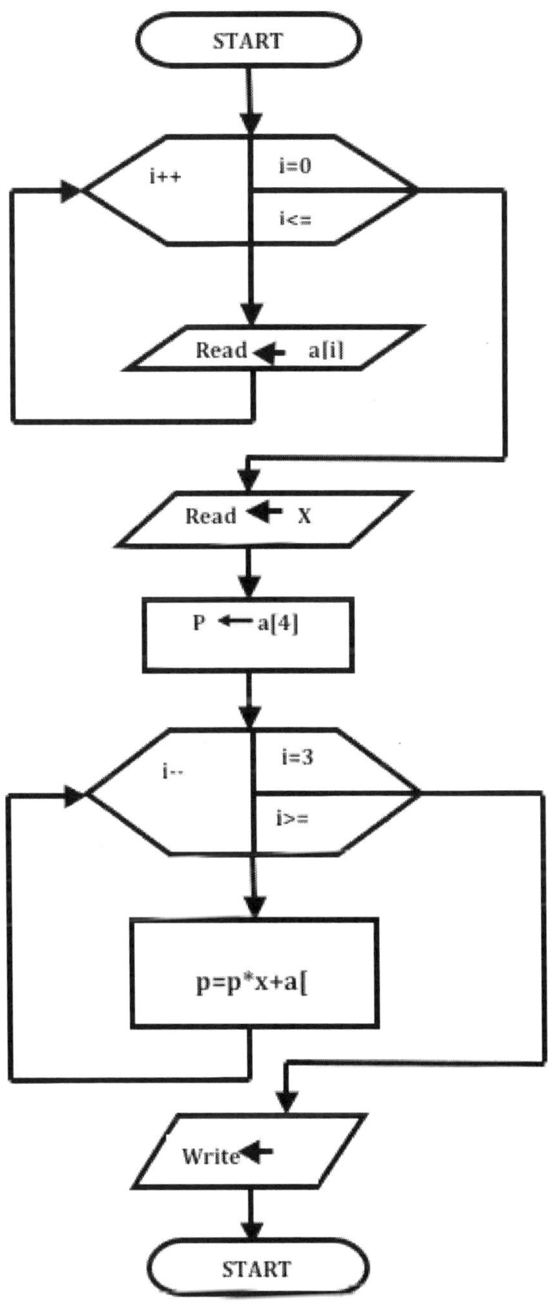

/* Program to find the Polynominal */

```
#include<stdio.h>
#include<conio.h>
void main( )
{
        int i,x,p,a[100];
        clrscr( );
        printf("Enter Five  elements");
        for(i=0;i<=4;i++)
        scanf("%d",&a[i]);
        printf("Enter the value of x\n");
        scanf("%d",&x);
        p=a[4];
        for(i=3;i>=0;i--)
        p=p*x+a[i];
        printf("The value of polynomial is=%d",p);
        getch( );
}
```

Output

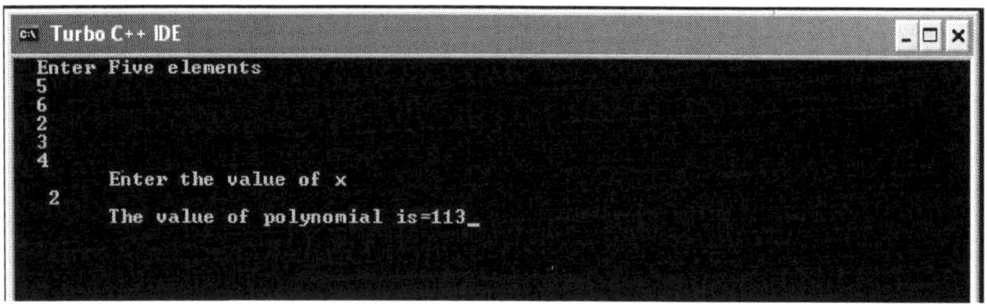

```
Turbo C++ IDE
Enter Five elements
5
6
2
3
4
        Enter the value of x
 2
        The value of polynomial is=113_
```

5. Draw the flowchart and Write a C Program to compute Sin(x) using Taylor series approximation given by Sin(x) = x - (x3/3!) + (x5/5!) - (x7/7!) + …….
Compare your result with the built- in Library function. Print both the results with appropriate messages.

Algorithm:

Step 1: Start

Step 2:read←n , degree // Read number of terms and x value in degree

Step 3: x←degree*3.142/180 //Convert x into radius.

term←x

sum←term

Step 4: //Calculate Sin series

for i=3 to n [increment by 2]

term← -term*x *x/(i*(i-1))

sum← sum+term

end for

Step 5://compare results

Write →sum

Write →sin (x)

Step 6: Stop

/* Flow Chart to compute Sin(x) using Taylor series */

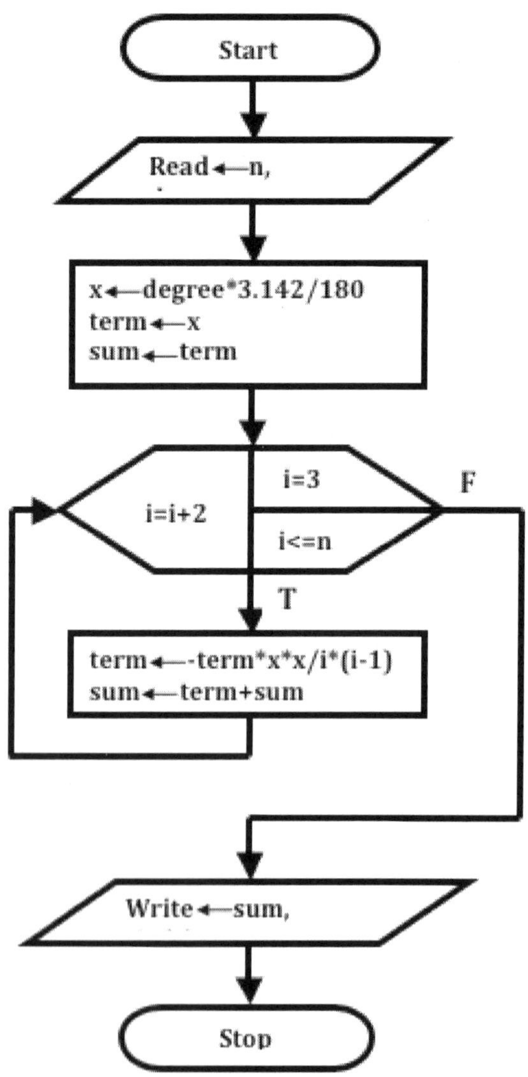

```
/* Program to compute Sin(x) using Taylor series */
#include<stdio.h>
#include<conio.h>
#include<math.h>
void main( )
{
        float term,degree,x,sum;
        int i,n;
        clrscr( );
        printf("\n enter the value in n\n");
        scanf("%d",&n);
        printf("\n enter the value in degree\n");
        scanf("%f",&degree);
        x=degree*3.142/180;
        term=x;
        sum=term;
        for(i=3;i<=n;i=i+2)
        {
                term=-term*x*x/(i*(i-1));
                sum=sum+term;
        }
        printf("the sin(x) is=%f\n",sum);
        printf("the sin(x) is=%f\n",sin(x));
        getch( );
}
```

Output

```
Turbo C++ IDE
 enter the value in n
 5

 enter the value in degree
 30
the sin(x) is=0.500061
the sin(x) is=0.500059
```

6. Develop an algorithm, implement and execute a C program that reads *N* integer numbers and arrange them in ascending order using *Bubble Sort*.

Algorithm:

Step 1:Start
Step 2: [Read Inputs]
read ← n
for i =0 to n
read ← a [i]
end for
Step 3: [given array]
for i =0 to n
Write →a [i] .
end for
Step 4:[sort the given array]
for i = 0 to n
for j = n-1 to i
if (a [j] < a [j-1])
exchange (a[j],a[j-1])
end if
end for j
end for i
Step 5: [sorted array]
for i = 0 to n
write→ a [i]
end for
Step 6: Stop.

Program:

```
#include<stdio.h>
#include<conio.h>
void main( )
{
        int i,j,n,temp;
        int a[100];
        clrscr();
```

```
        printf("enter size\n");
         scanf("%d",&n);
        printf("enter array\n");
        for(i=0;i<n;i++)
        scanf("%d",&a[i]);
        printf("Given array");
        for(i=0;i<n;i++)
        printf("\n%d",a[i]);
         for(i=0;i<n-1;i++)
        {
                for(j=n-1;j>i;j--)
                {
                        if(a[j]<a[j-1])
                        {
                            temp=a[j];
                            a[j]=a[j-1];
                            a[j-1]=temp;
                        }
                }
         }

        printf("\nThe sorted array is\n");
        for(i=0;i<n;i++)
        printf("%d\n",a[i]);
        getch( );
}
```

7. Develop, implement and execute a C program that reads two matrices *A* (m x n) and *B* (p x q) and Compute product of matrices *A* and *B*. Read matrix *A* and matrix *B* in row major order and in column major order respectively. Print both the input matrices and resultant matrix with suitable headings and output should be in matrix format only. Program must check the compatibility of orders of the matrices for multiplication. Report appropriate message in case of incompatibility.

Algorithm:

Step 1:Start

Step 2: [Read sizes of the matrices]

read ← m, n.
read ← p, q.

Step 3:[Check possibilities of multiplication]

if (n ! = p)
Not possibility of matrix multiplication.
end if.
Goto step 6.

Step 4:[Read the matrices]

read matrix A.
for i =0 to m
for j = 0 to n
read ← a [i] [j].
end for j.
end for i.
read matrix B.
for i =0 to p.
for j = 0 to q
read ← b [i] [j].
end for j.
end for i.

Step 5:[compute matrices multiplication]

for i =0 to m
for j = 0 to q
C [i][j] = 0
for k =0 to n.
c [i] [j] = c [i] [j + a [i] [k] * b [k] [j].

end for k.
end for j.
end for i.

Step 6: [Write matrices]
Write matrix A.
for i =0 to m
for j = 0 to n
write←a [i] [j]
end for j.
end for i.
Write matrix B.
for i =0 to p
for j = 0 to q
write←b [i] [j]
end for j.
end for i.
Write matrix c.
for i =0 to m.
for j = 0 to q
write←c [i] [j]
end for j.
end for i.
Step 7: stop.

Program:

```
#include<stdio.h>
#include<conio.h>
void main( )
{
        int i,j,k,m,n,p,q,a[10][10],b[10][10],c[10][10];
        clrscr( );
        printf("enter the size of matrix A\n");
        scanf("%d %d",&m,&n);
        printf("enter the size of matrix  B\n");
        scanf("%d %d",&p,&q);
```

```
if(n!=p)
 {
           printf("the product cannot be computed");
           getch( );
           exit(0);
 }

 printf("enter the elements of matrir A\n");
 for(i=0;i<m;i++)
 for(j=0;j<n;j++)
 scanf("%d",&a[i][j]);

 printf("enter the elements of matrix B\n");
 for(i=0;i<p;i++)
for(j=0;j<q;j++)
scanf("%d",&b[i][j]);

for(i=0;i<m;i++)
{
         for(j=0;j<q;j++)
         {
                  c[i][j]=0;
                  for(k=0;k<n;k++)
                  {
                           c[i][j]=c[i][j]+a[i][k]*b[k][j];
                  }
         }
}

printf("\nmatrix A is\n");
for(i=0;i<m;i++)
{
         for(j=0;j<n;j++)
         printf("%d ",a[i][j]);
         printf("\n");
}
```

```
        printf("\nmatrix B is\n");
        for(i=0;i<p;i++)
        {
                for(j=0;j<q;j++)
                printf("%d ",b[i][j]);
                printf("\n");
        }

        printf("\n Resultant matrix C is\n");
        for(i=0;i<m;i++)
        {
                for(j=0;j<q;j++)
                printf("%d ",c[i][j]);
                printf("\n");
        }
        getch( );
}
```

8. Develop, implement and execute a C program to search a Name in a list of names using *Binary searching* Technique.

Algorithm:

Step 1: Start

Step 2: read←n

for i=0 to i<n [increment by 1]

read ← a[i]

end for

read ← key

end for

Step 3: low← 0

high← n-1

found=1

Step 4:while(low<=high && !found)

mid=low+high/2

if(strcmp(arr[mid] , key)==0)

found=1

else if(strcmp(arr[mid],key)<0)

else

high=mid-1

end while

if(found==1)

write→search successful

else

write→unsuccessful search

Step 5: Stop

Program:

```
#include<stdio.h>
#include<conio.h>
#include<stdlib.h>
void main()
{
	char  arr[25][20], key[25];
	int i, n,low,high,mid, cond;
	clrscr( );
	printf("Enter the number of strings you want to enter\n");
	scanf("%d", &n);
	printf("Enter %d strings\n", n);
	for (i=0; i<n; i++)
	{
		scanf("%s", arr[i]);
	}
	printf("Entered String are\n");
	for(i=0; i<n; i++)
	{
		printf("%s\n", arr[i]);
	}
	printf("\n");

	printf("Enter string to be searched\n");
	scanf("%s", key);
	low = 0;
	high= n-1;

	while(low <= high)
	{
		mid = (low + high) / 2;
		if((cond = strcmp(arr[mid], key)) == 0)
```

```
            {
                    printf("Key found at %d position", mid+1);
                    getch();
                    exit(0);
            }
            else if(cond < 0)
            low = mid + 1;
            else
            high = mid - 1;
        }
        printf("String is not found\n");
        getch( );
        return 0;
}
```

9. Write and execute a C program that
i. Implements string copy operation *STRCOPY*(str1,str2) that copies a string *str1* to another string *str2* without using library function.

Algorithm:

Step 1: Start

Step 2: read←str1

Step 3:STRCOPY(str1,str2)

Step 4: write→str2

Step 5:Stop

//Function STRCOPY(str1 , str2)

Step 1: Start

Step 2: i=0 ,j=0

Step 3: while (str1[i]!='\0')

Str2[i]←str[i]

j++

i++

end while

Step 4:return

Step 5:Stop

Program:

```
#include<stdio.h>
#include<conio.h>
void strcopy(char str1[100],char str2[100]);
void main()
```

```
{
char str1[100],str2[100];
clrscr();
printf("\n Enter the string \n");
gets(str1);
printf("\n Entered string is \n");
puts(str1);
strcopy(str1,str2);
printf("\n The copied string is:\n");
puts(str2);
getch();
}

void strcopy(char str1[100],char str2[100])
{
int i=0,j=0;
while(str1[i]!='\0')
{
        str2[j]=str1[i];
        j++;
        i++;
}
str2[j]='\0';
}
```

ii. Read a *sentence* and print frequency of vowels and total count of consonants.

Algorithm :

Step 1: Start

Step 2: read←string
        i=0
Step 3: while (string[i]='\0')
        Switch(string[i])
        Case 'a': a++
        Case 'A':
                break
                goto step 3
        case 'e': e++
        case 'E':
                break
                goto step 3
        case 'i': i++
        case 'I':
                break
                goto step 3
        case 'o': i++
        case 'O':
                break
                goto stcp 3
        case 'u': i++
        case 'U':
                break
                goto step 3

        default: consonants + 1
                end switch
                end while

Step 4: return← a, e ,i ,o, u count and consonant count

Step 5:Stop

Program:

```
#include<stdio.h>
#include<conio.h>
int main(void) {
   char str[100];
   int i=0, acnt=0, ecnt=0, icnt=0, ocnt=0, ucnt=0, vcnt=0;
   clrscr();
   printf("Enter the sentence\n");
   gets(str);
   while(str[i]!='\0') {
         switch(str[i]) {
            case 'A':
            case 'a': acnt++;
                     break;
            case 'E':
            case 'e': ecnt++;
                     break;
            case 'I':
            case 'i': icnt++;
                     break;
            case 'O':
            case 'o': ocnt++;
                     break;
            case 'U':
            case 'u': ucnt++;
                     break;
            default : vcnt++;
         }
         i++;
   }
   printf("A vowel count is %d\n", acnt);
   printf("E vowel count is %d\n", ecnt);
   printf("I vowel count is %d\n", icnt);
   printf("O vowel count is %d\n", ocnt);
   printf("U vowel count is %d\n", ucnt);
   printf("Constants count is %d\n", vcnt);
   getch();
   return 0;
}
```

10.

a. Design and develop a C function *RightShift(x ,n)* that takes two integers *x* and *n* as input and returns value of the integer *x* rotated to the right by *n* positions. Assume the integers are unsigned. Write a C program that invokes this function with different values for *x* and *n* and tabulate the results with suitable headings.

Algorithm :

```
# define MSBVALUE 32768
Step 1: [Read Inputs]
        While (1)
        begin
                Read← x.
                Read ← n.
                        Result ← rightrot(x , n). {goto step A1}.
        End while.
Step2:[Display results].
                Write→ result (x).
                Read ← Y or N.
                If Y goto step1.
                If N goto step 3.
Step3: stop
StepA1:[Function Right rot]
        For i = 0 to n
                Rem← x%2.
                If ( rem==0)                    X = x >> 1.
                Else
                                                X = x >> 1;
X= x + MSBVALUE.
                End if.
        Return x.
End for.
Step A2: stop.
```

Program:

```
#include<stdio.h>
```

```
#include<conio.h>
#define MSBVALUE 32768
unsigned int righrot(unsigned int x,int n)
{
int rem,i;
clrscr();
for (i=1;i<=n;i++)
{
        rem=x%2;
        if(rem==0)
        {
                x = x >> 1;
        }
        else
        {
                x = x >>  1;
                x = x + MSBVALUE;
        }
}
return(x);
}
void main()
 {
  unsigned int x,result;
  int n;
  char ch;
  clrscr();
  while(1)
  {
   printf("\n\nEnter number which is to rotated:");
   scanf("%u",&x);
   printf("\n\nEnter how many bits to be rotated:");
   scanf("%d",&n);
   result=righrot(x,n);
    printf("\n\nright rotation of %u by %d is %u",x,n,result);
   printf("\n\n Do U WANT TO CONTINUE\n type 'y' for yes 'n'
for no:");
   scanf(" %c",&ch);
   if(ch=='N'||ch=='n')
```

```
  break;
 }
getch();
}
```

b. Design and develop a C function isprime(num) that accepts an integer argument and returns 1 if the argument is prime, a 0 otherwise. Write a C program that invokes this function to generate prime numbers between the given range.

Algorithm:

```
Step 1:Start
Step 2:read ←low,high
Step 3:for i=low to high
            i←isprime( i )
           if(i==1)
           i→write
           end for
Step 4:Stop
//Function on isprime(num)
Step 1:Start
Step 2:for(i=2;i<=n/2;i++)
        If((num%i)==0)
                return ←0
        else
                return  n← 1
        end for
Step 3:Stop
```

Program:

```
#include<stdio.h>
#include<conio.h>
int flag = 1;
int isprime(int x) {
   int i;
   for(i=2; i<=x/2; i++) {
          if(x%i == 0) {
             flag = 0;
```

```
            break;
        }
    }
    return flag;
}
int main() {
    int low, high, i, r;
    clrscr();
    printf("enter a number greater than 0\n");
    scanf("%d %d", &low, &high);
    for(i=low; i<=high; i++) {
        r = isprime(i);
        if(r == 1)
            printf("%d ", i);
        else
// Reset flag value because value of flag is set to zero when a
number is not prime
            flag=1;
    }
    getch();
    }
```

11. Draw the flowchart and write a recursive C function to find the factorial of a number,n!, defined by fact(n)=1, if n=0. Otherwise fact(n)=n*fact(n-1). Using this function,write a C program to compute the binomial coefficient nCr. Tabulate the results for different values of n and r with suitable messages.

Algorithm:

Step 1:Start

Step 2:read n , r

Step 3: result←(fact (n)/(fact(n-r) * fact(r)))

Step 4:write→result

//Function to find factorial of number

Step 1:Start

Step 2:if n is 0 then

return 1

else

return (n*fact(n))

Step 3:Stop

Program:

```
#include<stdio.h>
#include<conio.h>
int fact(int x);
void main()
{
int n,r,ncr;
clrscr();
printf(" Enter the n value \n");
```

```
scanf("%d",&n);
printf(" Enter the value R \n");
scanf("%d",&r);
ncr=fact(n)/(fact(n-r)*fact(r));
printf("The result of nCr is %d \n",ncr);
getch();
}
int fact(int x)
{
 if(x==0)
        return 1;
 else
        return (x*fact(x-1));
}
```

12. Given two university information files "studentname.txt" and "usn.txt" that contains students Name and USN respectively. Write a C program to create a new file called "output.txt" and copy the content of files "studentname.txt" and "usn.txt" into output file in the sequence shown below . Display the contents of output file "output.txt" on to the screen.

Student Name	USN
Name 1	USN1
Name 2	USN2
....	....
....	....

Heading (→ Student Name / USN row)

Algorithm :

Step 1: Start
Step 2: FILE *fp1 , *fp2 ,*fp3
 fp1← fopen("name.text","r")
 fp2← fopen("USN.text","r")
 fp3← fopen("output.text","w")
Step 3:if (fp1=NULL or fp2== NULL)
 Write→ unable to open a file
 Goto step 5
Step 4:while(fgets(s1 , 80 ,fp1)!==NULL and fgets(s2 , 80 ,fp2)!==NULL))
 S3=='\0' // mark null
 Strcat(s3,s1) //copy the s1 to s3 , here s3 contains name , so now usn will copy after name
 fprint(s3 , fp3) // s3 will copy or print to file output
Step 5:Stop

Program:

```
#include<stdio.h>
#include<conio.h>
void main()
```

```
{
FILE *fp1,*fp2,*fp3;
char s1[80],s2[80],s3[80];
clrscr();
fp1=fopen("name.txt","r");
fp2=fopen("usn.txt","r");
fp3=fopen("output.txt","w");
clrscr();
if(fp1==NULL||fp2==NULL)
{
printf("unable to open");
getch();
exit(0);
}
printf("students name \t USN \n");
while((fgets(s1,80,fp1))!=NULL&&(fgets(s2,80,fp2)!=NULL))
{
s3[0]='\0';
strcat(s3,s1);
s3[strlen(s3)-1]='\t';
strcat(s3,s2);
fputs(s3,fp3);
printf("%s",s3);
fputs(s3,fp3);
fcloseall();
getch();
}
}
```

13. Write a C program to maintain a record of n student details using an array of structures with four fields (Roll number, Name, Marks, and Grade). Assume appropriate data type for each field. Print the marks of the student, given the student name as input.

Algorithm:

Step 1: Start
Step 2: read ← structural member values
    for i←0 to n [increment by 1]
    read← s[i].name
    read← s[i].rollno.
    read← s[i].marks
    read← s[i].grade
    end for
Step 3: read key element name
    read← keyname
Step 4: if (strcmp(s[i].name , keyname)==0)
    found=1
Step 5:if(found==0)
    Write→ name does not exist
Step 6:Stop

Program:

```
#include<stdio.h>
#include<conio.h>
#include<string.h>
void main()
{
struct student
{
int rollno;
char name[20];
int marks;
char grade[1];
};
struct student s[100],t;
```

```
int i,j,n,a,flag=0;
char name[20];
clrscr();
printf("\n enter the limit");
scanf("%d",&n);
for(i=0;i<n;i++)
{
printf("\n enter the roll no\n");
scanf("%d",&s[i].rollno);
printf("\n enter the name \n");
scanf("%s",s[i].name);
printf("\n enter the mark =");
scanf("%d",&s[i].marks);
printf("\n enter the grade =");
scanf("%s",s[i].grade);
}
printf("\n enter the name \n");
scanf("%s",name);
for(i=0;i<n;i++)
{
a=strcmp(s[i].name,name);
if(a==0)
{
flag=1;
printf("\n rollno=%d",s[i].rollno);
printf("\n name=%s",s[i].name);
printf("\n marks=%d",s[i].marks);
printf("\n grade=%s",s[i].grade);
}}
if(flag==1)
printf("\n  the student  found \n");
else
printf("student not found");
getch();
}
```

14. Write a C program using pointers to compute the sum, mean and standard deviation of all elements stored in an array of n real numbers.

Algorithm:

Step 1: Start
Step 2: read ←n //number of elements.
Step 3: read←x[i]
  for i← 0 to n [increment by 1]
  read← x[i]
  end for
Step 4: assign array to pointer
  ptr=x
Step 5: for i<0 to n
  Sum←sum + *ptr
  End for
Step 6: calculate mean
  mean←sum/n
Step 7: for i=0 to n [increment by 1]
  Stddiv_sum← stddivsum+ pow((*ptr-mean),2)
  End for
Step 8: stddiv← sqrt(stddiv_sum/n)
Step 9: write→sum
  write→mean
  write→stddiv
Step 10:Stop

Program:

```
#includc <stdio.h>
#include <math.h>
#define MAXSIZE 10
void main()
{
   float x[MAXSIZE];
   int i, n;
   float average, variance, std_deviation, sum = 0, sum1 = 0;
   printf("Enter the value of N \n");
   scanf("%d", &n);
```

```
    printf("Enter %d real numbers \n", n);
    for (i = 0; i < n; i++)
    {
        scanf("%f", &x[i]);
    }
    /* Compute the sum of all elements */
    for (i = 0; i < n; i++)
    {
        sum = sum + x[i];
    }
    average = sum / (float)n;
    /* Compute variance and standard deviation */
    for (i = 0; i < n; i++)
    {
        sum1 = sum1 + pow((x[i] - average), 2);
    }
    variance = sum1 / (float)n;
    std_deviation = sqrt(variance);
    printf("Average of all elements = %.2f\n", average);
    printf("variance of all elements = %.2f\n", variance);
    printf("Standard deviation = %.2f\n", std_deviation);
}
```

References

1. C Programming Language Dennis Ritchie, Brian W. Kernighan
2. The C Answer Book by Tondo
3. Let Us C – 14TH Edition by Yashavant Kanetkar
4. The Complete Reference by Herbert Schildt
5. C Programming Language: The Ultimate Guide for Beginners
6. C Language Tutorials URL: www.tutorialspoint.com
7. Easy C Programming for Beginners, Your Step-By-Step Guide To Learning C Programming (C Programming Series) by Felix Alvaro
8. Let Us C Solutions by Yashavant P. Kanetkar